Chasing Butterflies

YEJIDE KILANKO

This book contains an excerpt from the novel *Daughters Who Walk This Path*. Copyright © 2012 by Yejide Kilanko.

E-Book ISBN: 978-0-9950361-3-0

Paperback ISBN: 978-0-9950361-2-3

Ayoka Books, Ontario, Canada.

Copyright © 2017 by Yejide Kilanko

www.yejidekilanko.com

by the same author

DAUGHTERS WHO WALK THIS PATH

DEDICATION

To Oladele

You truly ease my troubles.

CHAPTER ONE

Under the spotlight, all Tomide Ojo could see from the stage was a faint outline of his wife's face. He'd thought Titilope would vanish through the shiny hardwood floors when he told her he was going to sign up for an open mic spot.

Tomide balanced the guitar on his lap and pulled the microphone close. "This is for my beautiful wife, Titilope. Happy Valentine's Day, darling. Here's to sweeter days."

He smiled when Titilope covered her face with both hands. Tomide strummed the guitar to an acoustic version of Timi Dakolo's "*Iyawo Mi.*" As his voice filled the room, Titilope's face blurred.

When things became serious between them, he'd been upfront about what he wanted from a wife. His expectations were not unrealistic. Bottom line, he wanted a woman who knew how to take care of a man the proper way. The way his mother had taken care of his father. Titilope agreed to the terms, only to change after he'd placed a wedding band on her finger. Any sensible person would agree that Titilope's behaviour was a breach of contract. To be fair, there'd been some good moments. He was also grateful for their son.

Tomide stood up from the stage stool and finished the song with flourish. He took a bow and stepped off the stage to enthusiastic whistles and applause. *And that's how to make a romantic statement,* Tomide thought as he walked towards Titilope with hands stuck in his pockets.

"Welcome back, Mr. Superstar," Titilope said dryly as he took a seat beside her.

He leaned into her. "I remembered our song."

She rolled her eyes. *"Darling,* that was sweet of you."

Tomide grinned. They normally didn't use terms of endearment. Up on the stage, it had felt like the right thing to say.

The silence between them stretched as Titilope stared into her glass of water. "So, what did you think of my performance?"

Titilope bit hard on her lower lip. It was what she did when she didn't know what to say or felt the need to embellish the truth. "It was…nice."

Nice was just another word for mediocre. "That's all you've got?"

She held his gaze. "Tomide, love is more than grand gestures."

Her melancholy was beginning to grate on his nerves. "I don't do anything in half measures."

Titilope's eyes clouded over. "No, you don't."

Determined to hold on to his good mood, Tomide took a deep breath. "The plan was for us to have a fun, child-free weekend. We can sit here and rehash old issues or move to the dance floor and have some fun. Your choice."

"If only it could always be like this," Titilope said in a wistful tone.

He gave an emphatic nod. "It can be."

Titilope snorted. "It can?"

He still believed so. "Things just get messy when we both forget to play our part."

She searched his face and then visibly pulled herself together. "It would be a shame to waste our dinner and dance coupon."

Tomide held out his hand. Titilope took it. "That's my penny-pinching girl," he said with a smile.

CHAPTER TWO

The sensation of moist air against Titilope's earlobe woke her up. She opened her eyes and saw T.J. standing over her.

"Mum, we're leaving," he said.

Titilope lifted her head, frowning when she spotted an oily smudge on the textbook page she had been reading. The book had been borrowed from their public library.

"Are you okay?" T.J. asked.

She forced a smile. "Yes, sweetie."

T.J. grinned when she reached out and rubbed his head. He was going to spend the night at his brother's. "Did you bring down your backpack?"

He slapped his forehead. "I forgot."

She stifled a big yawn. "Go and get it."

Tomide, who'd been standing to the side checking his wallet, spoke after T.J. left the room. "Madam, is this how you intend to study?"

Her CPA certification exams were only a week away. She still had a lot of material to cover. "I keep nodding off."

Tomide looked at her thoughtfully. "*Abi*, you've swallowed a cockroach?"

Her stomach turned as she imagined the despised insect sliding down her throat. "What kind of person eats a cockroach?"

Tomide chuckled. "I forgot you're an *ajebutter* city girl."

She pushed back her chair and stood up. "Here we go again with the sob stories. Like you didn't eat butter as a child."

"Me? *Who dash monkey banana?* I'm just wondering if you're pregnant."

The thought of a baby made Titilope's heart skip. Her periods were out of sync and she had developed a strange craving for Brussels sprouts. She had thought it was all due to stress.

Her eyes settled on Tomide's calm face. While he seemed fine with the idea of another child, for her, it would be a major disaster.

Tomide slid his wallet into his pocket. "Take a walk around the neighbourhood. The fresh air might clear your head."

Her hands trembled as she packed up her books. "I'll do that."

After Tomide and T.J. left the house, she grabbed her purse, drove to their neighbourhood pharmacy and bought five pregnancy test kits.

Behind the locked bathroom door, she dipped the fifth test wand in the urine-filled container, set it down on the counter and waited for the required three minutes. She got the same beautiful result. NOT PREGNANT. Titilope rested her back against the countertop.

"Titilope, where are you?"

The sound of Tomide's voice sent her into a panic. She shoved the boxes and wrappers into a plastic bag and hid it under the sink.

"I'm in the bathroom."

"I need to talk to you," Tomide said from the other side of the door.

What could he want? "I'm almost done."

"I'll be in the living room."

Titilope flushed the toilet and took some calming breaths before she washed her hands and face. After a quick look in the mirror, she hurried to the living room. "Hey."

Tomide turned away from the television. "Kazeem called on my drive back home. The crazy man's throwing a surprise fortieth birthday party for his wife. I told him we'd attend."

It wasn't the first time Tomide had confirmed their attendance at an event without discussing it with her. If she dared to make such a commitment, it would be war.

Tomide peered at her face. "Are you okay?"

The adrenaline rush she'd experienced at the sound of his voice had left her covered in sweat. "I think I need a proper nap."

Tomide shook his head. "What you need to do is study. We can't afford another repeat exam."

Based on how her textbook sentences merged and mutated into random information, failure was a scary possibility.

"I won't need one." The tremor in her voice suggested otherwise.

"I hope so. Before I forget, the boys are coming to watch a game later in the day. I checked, and there wasn't anything interesting in the fridge."

Titilope's anger rose as she shifted from one foot to the other. During basketball season, the boys – Tomide's friends – watched most of the games at their house. "You can order pizza and chicken wings," she said.

Tomide winked. "Not when they know there's a five-star cook in the house."

She loved to cook. It relaxed her. She just didn't like how Tomide invited anybody who was looking for somewhere to go just so he could play generous host at her expense.

"There's nothing wrong with you making a meal for your friends."

"You're funny." He picked up the television remote. "Go and take your nap. I'll wake you in an hour."

Titilope stood for a while as she debated what to do. A strategic back door escape to the library or kitchen duties?

"Time's going," Tomide said.

She glared at him for several more seconds before she stomped her way to the bedroom. One day, he was going to push her too far.

***

Titilope pulled the new firefighter bedding set out of its plastic bag. It matched T.J.'s fire-engine red bed.

T.J.'s eyes lit up as she shook it out. "That's so cool," he said.

She smiled. Cool was his new favourite word. "I'm glad you like it."

T.J. who had been putting away his folded clothes came over and gave her a hug. "Thanks, Mum."

She took a deep breath as her arms tightened around his little body. She felt that she was at least doing some things right. "You're welcome, my love. I also bought you some snacks. Go and get your bin."

After she had restocked T.J.'s emergency food bin, she decided that they'd done enough work for the evening. It was a school night.

T.J. had brushed his teeth before she tucked him in bed. "Sleep tight. Don't let the bedbugs bite."

T.J. laughed. "Dad said bedbugs couldn't live here. They don't have money."

Tomide wasn't a fan of moochers. "You know your father. Rent payers only."

"But, I don't pay rent," T.J said.

"You don't need to. Your hugs and kisses are more valuable than money." She rubbed his head before she switched off his bedroom light and closed the door. She had a few things to do before she could go to bed.

Titilope packed their lunch bags with some snacks, made sandwiches, wiped down the kitchen counters and loaded the dishwasher before she headed outside. On her way in, she'd neglected to check the mailbox. The lone piece of mail in the box had her name on it. Her pulse quickened when she saw that it came from the Maryland State Board of Public Accountancy.

Back inside their brick townhouse, she tore open the envelope, quickly read the letter and danced her way from the foyer to the living room. "Tomide!"

He came up from his basement man cave. "What's going on?"

She held out the letter. "I passed my exams."

Tomide scanned through the document before he gave her a tight hug. "I'm getting closer to early retirement and a house husband role."

She stepped back for a clearer view of his face. "You? A house husband?"

Tomide grinned. "I'll be quite content to stay home to clean and cook while you make the big bucks; bye-bye, Nine to Five, hello, life of luxury."

Mr. Husband certainly had an interesting view about what she did all day. "Did you just say clean and cook?"

Tomide nodded. "You these abroad women always make housework sound so complicated. You have a dishwasher, a washing machine, uninterrupted water, and light. Your counterparts back home have way less, and they don't disturb their men."

What Tomide failed to recognise was that women back home in Nigeria often had helpers. "Your last visit to Lagos was what, eight or nine years ago? *Bros*, life has changed."

Tomide snickered. "The truth is God equipped men and women for different tasks. Before you carry a protest placard with my name stamped on it, remember that nature decided that. And the sooner you and your gang of angry women accept that, the better for us all."

Her teeth clenched as she swallowed her words. It wasn't the night for an argument.

As she tried to move away, Tomide swung his arm around her shoulders. "This calls for a celebration. Is there a particular restaurant the newly board certified accountant wants to visit?"

"I'll think about it. Right now, all I want is a long bath and two glasses of wine before I snuggle in my one-piece flannel pyjamas."

Tomide scowled. "That onesie of yours is a romance killer."

Titilope kept a straight face. That was why she wore it.

He pulled her close. "Hey, there's wine in the upstairs mini fridge. And I'm quite good with a loofah. If you find my service helpful, perhaps I can influence your nightwear choice?"

She lifted her chin. "You will have to use some top-notch persuasive skills."

He pointed in the direction of the staircase. "I like a challenge. After you, madam."

CHAPTER THREE

At the sound of Bunmi's voice, she turned off the answering machine and picked up the phone. "Hey, friend."

"Madam Titilope. *Na wa* o. Are you people now screening calls?"

"Yes *ke*. We're not taking calls from pesky Laurel residents."

"*Yeye* Rockville woman," Bunmi said with a cackle. "Are you home this afternoon? James and I were thinking of stopping by."

With T.J. at a birthday party, she'd planned to shop for groceries. But since it was Bunmi, shopping could wait. "I'm home. I'll check in with Tomide and call you back."

"Sounds good. Talk to you soon."

Titilope held on to the phone as she faced her husband. "That was Bunmi. Is it okay for them to visit?"

Tomide kept his gaze on the television. "James is always welcome at my house."

His blatant animosity towards Bunmi puzzled her. "What has she done to you?"

Tomide glanced at her. "She turned my friend into her doormat."

Titilope found Bunmi's comfortable relationship with her husband enviable. "Remember she played matchmaker for you."

Tomide snorted. "She did introduce us. But I sealed the deal."

As far she was concerned, their marriage now felt like a hostile takeover.

Titilope turned away, dialled Bunmi's number and told her friend that they couldn't wait to see them. It was her home too.

***

Titilope was in their bedroom when the doorbell rang. Tomide answered the door. At the sound of James' laughter, she hurried down the stairs. Arms wide open, she walked towards Bunmi. "*Ore mi*. It's so good to see you," she said.

Bunmi gave her a tight hug. "Your face has been scarce."

"*Ma binu*. I didn't know adult education was so hard."

"See how fast you were able to get an accounting job! It all paid off."

"The next step is to get a better paying job," Titilope said.

"One will come." Bunmi turned to Tomide. "How's life in Tomideville?"

Tomide tilted his head. "Things are quite well in the kingdom. Long live the King."

"More like long live the despot," Bunmi said with a sweet smile.

Tomide's expression soured.

Titilope was glad when James stepped between them. James lowered his head in mock deference as he held out a glittery wine bag. "Something to wet the King's parched throat," he said.

Tomide smiled. "My man."

"As my people say, 'He who brings wine brings happiness'."

Tomide accepted the bag from James. "So does he who brings a Ghana-must-go bag filled with crisp bundles of money. However, in the spirit of our long-standing friendship, for today, the wine will do."

James patted him on the back. "Well spoken, my brother."

Tomide led their guests from the foyer to the living room. At his request, Titilope went to the kitchen and brought back an ice bucket and wine glasses. "I made some Jollof rice," she said.

Tomide uncorked the bottle of wine. "*Abeg*, rice is for birds. I'm sure they'll prefer to swallow some pounded yam and *egusi* soup."

Bunmi exchanged a look with her husband.

"Since I'm working on my six pack, a light snack is fine," James said with a bright smile.

"I'll make us some chicken kebabs," Titilope said before Tomide could speak. "Protein and veggies will be good for you."

Bunmi stood up. "That's perfect. Four hands will make the work lighter."

Titilope smiled at her friend as they walked through the open concept space to the kitchen area. "The kebabs are pre-cooked. I only have to put them in the oven."

"I didn't come here to create more work for you," Bunmi said.

Titilope stopped in front of the standing freezer. "Do you hear any complaints from me?" As she opened the freezer door, Bunmi, who had been trying to get out of her way, bumped an elbow into her ribcage. Titilope gave a little cry.

Bunmi stepped back. "Are you okay?"

She leaned against the counter and tried to smile through the pain. "Yes."

Bunmi's eyes widened. "You're bleeding."

Titilope looked down and saw the blood stain. The contact with Bunmi's elbow had re-opened a scabbed over wound. "It's no big deal," she said.

Bunmi lowered her voice. "What happened?"

Titilope forced another smile. "Don't mind me. I keep running into things and hurting myself."

Bunmi's expression grew pensive. "*Ore*, I'm worried about you. When we lived together, you didn't have all these accidents. Is there something you need to tell me?"

Woman, don't you get carried away. "Honestly, there's nothing," she said.

"Whatever's going on, we can deal with it."

To keep them from being overheard, Titilope turned on the tap. "You journalists and your wild imaginations."

"I'm serious. You and T.J. are always welcome at our home. James would not let my best friend sleep on the streets."

"A good mother does not run from her child's home. She always stays and fights."

Bunmi snorted. "*Abeg*. Who told you such nonsense?"

She tore off a paper towel and held it under the running tap. "There's nothing for you to worry about."

"No matter how many times you say it, I don't believe you." Bunmi walked out of the kitchen area.

How could Bunmi understand her situation? She had a husband who adored her. Tomide already said she was a mediocre wife. She couldn't be a bad mother too.

After she'd dabbed at the bloodstain and most of it was out, Titilope washed her hands and brought out the bag of kebabs. The skewers were arranged in a roasting pan and placed in the oven. She turned on the timer and took another look at the wet spot on her blouse. Thanks to the chiffon fabric, it wasn't that bad.

When she returned to the living room, Tomide patted the spot beside him. When she sat down, he placed a warm hand on her thigh. "Do you remember the encounter I had with the police when we travelled back to Nigeria for our wedding?" he asked.

Conscious of Bunmi's glare, she got rid of Tomide's hand by crossing her legs. "What encounter?"

"The one at Alabata bus stop."

"Oh."

She stared at Tomide as he told their guests yet another version of the story she first heard during their honeymoon.

The storytelling took Tomide to the edge of his seat. "I was driving my mother's car when I ran into a police checkpoint. I knew there was trouble when his '*oga wetin you carry*' led to the demand for a government issued car plate receipt. When I said I didn't have one, the officer opened the passenger door and jumped in. He said I had to take him to their station."

James leaned forward when Tomide paused and took a sip of his wine. Bunmi's face remained frozen.

Titilope nervously smoothed the flared skirt over her legs as she wondered if she could excuse herself to sit in the kitchen.

Tomide smacked his lips. "During our drive to the police station, I pulled out my cell phone, dialled a random number and started a conversation with dead air. I said, 'Baba, I *don* catch the last one. Yes, we now have all the fresh heads needed.'"

James clapped. "*Chai*! Tomide, *you be mad man.*"

Tomide chuckled. "I then said to the imaginary Baba, '*We dey come now-now, make you prepare ground.*'"

The expression on James' face swung between disbelief and admiration. "Didn't the officer have his gun?"

"It was strapped to his side. The fool didn't remember he had it or maybe there were no bullets. He just kept begging me to drop him off. You should have seen my smile when I asked him, '*Oga, you dey fear? Na station we dey go.*' After I parked the car and told him to get out, he took off like someone running from his creditors."

James gave his friend a fist bump. "*Cunny* man die, *cunny* man bury am."

Tomide nodded. "He saw my fresh face and thought he'd found a *mugu*. Common thief."

The ding of the oven timer made Titilope jump up from her seat. "The kebabs are ready."

An hour later, they walked their guests to their car. Bunmi placed a hand on Titilope's arm as the men strolled ahead. Titilope slowed her pace. "What?"

"Promise you'll call if you need help," Bunmi said.

She should have known Bunmi wouldn't drop the subject. "Do you now run a 911 service?"

Bunmi looked exasperated. "Titilope, I'm serious."

Titilope lowered her voice. "Me too. There's nothing to worry about."

Bunmi hissed the words. "Promise me."

The men stopped walking. Tomide glanced over his shoulder. She'd better end the conversation. "Fine. I'll call you if something comes up."

As Bunmi hugged her, Titilope told herself she didn't need saving. It was her life, her mess.

CHAPTER FOUR

The shrill sound of the doorbell made Titilope switch off the vacuum cleaner; through the peephole she saw a slim, blue-eyed woman and a little boy. Even now, the resemblance between Tomide and his elder son was amazing. She opened the door with a smile. "Hello, guys."

Jordan stepped into the house. "Hi, Aunty Titilope."

"Hello, my dear. T.J. has been waiting for you."

Jordan shot his mother a pointed look. "It was Mum's fault. She made me eat a healthy meal before we left home."

Titilope laughed at Holly's embarrassed expression. "I guess she doesn't like our candy pizza nights."

Jordan rubbed his stomach. "They're yummy."

Holly kept a straight face. "Well, you've had dinner. So, no candy pizzas, no sodas, and definitely no playing video games past midnight."

Titilope folded arms across her chest. "Hey, this is my house. You can have all those Grinch rules over at your place."

Jordan stepped around her and ran towards the stairs. "T.J., I'm here!"

T.J. ran out of his room onto the landing. "Dude, I've been waiting for you!"

Titilope shook her head. Both boys lacked indoor voices. Holly had said it was their Nigerianness. She had expressed her disagreement in a loud voice.

Holly turned to her after Jordan bounced up the stairs. "You spoil him."

"Relax. I'll make sure to serve tofu sandwiches and vegetable juice for night snacks. And they'll be in bed by 9 p.m. If you believe me…"

Holly laughed. "You're so wrong."

Titilope winked. "I have to work hard for my Aunty title."

"So, I heard someone passed their exam," Holly said.

"Who told you?"

"Those two upstairs tell each other everything."

Titilope hoped there were some things T.J. kept to himself. "I'm so glad it's all over."

Holly opened her purse and brought out an envelope. "Since you let all the flowers I bring die, I thought a spa certificate would be a more useful present."

Titilope took the envelope and did a double take at the embossed lettering. *Vivant* was a premier downtown spa. "You didn't have to get me anything."

"I wanted to. You worked hard for this. Really proud of you."

"Thank you."

"You're welcome," Holly said as they exchanged warm smiles.

Bunmi often told her that the relationship with Holly was peculiar; that Holly might as well be her senior co-wife but Titilope knew that Holly would gag at the thought of them sharing Tomide.

Their relationship had gotten off to a shaky start. She still remembered Holly's snarky tone as she asked if Titilope was 'the woman Tomide found', as though she were an item discovered in a bargain store bin.

T.J.'s birth changed things between them. She was touched when Holly brought Jordan to the hospital in a T-shirt with the words, "Kiss Me, I'm the Big Brother." Jordan had placed his gift; a giant stuffed panda, at the foot of T.J.'s crib and spent the hour-long visit enthralled by him. Jordan's name was one of T.J.'s first words. For their sons' sake, they had learned to be cordial. The mutual respect and affection came naturally as they shared their lives.

Holly glanced at her wristwatch. "Well, my book club waits. I'll see you all on Sunday afternoon. That'll be around one?"

"How about I call when Jordan's ready to come home. There's a travelling zoo coming to the mall this weekend. T.J. wants to go. I'm sure Jordan would love it."

"Fine by me. I wouldn't say no to more sleep."

Titilope turned to the landing. "Jordan, your mum's leaving! She needs a big hug from you."

Jordan's protest was loud and clear. "Oh no, not again!"

She and Holly looked at each other and laughed.

***

Tomide opened the front door and walked into the open concept space. "I'm home."

Titilope who had been standing by the kitchen island chopping vegetables for a stir-fry spoke first. "Welcome."

Tomide's response was drowned out by Jordan's squeal. He jumped off the couch and ran towards Tomide. "Dad!"

Tomide gave him a high five. "J-Man!"

T.J. greeted Tomide. "Welcome, Dad." He didn't get a response. Tomide stayed focused on his older son.

Titilope's heart ached for T.J. as he stared at his brother and father. *Mr. Man, open your eyes. Can't you see what you're doing to your son?*

Tomide walked over to the kitchen and washed his hands. "How was your day?" he asked her.

Her fingers gripped the knife handle. "Fine."

Tomide tossed the paper towel he wiped his hand with into the trash can. "Good."

He joined T.J. and Jordan on the couch. "Boys, I wanna hear about your day."

Titilope found the way Tomide's accent changed during Jordan's visits amusing. Every other sentence suddenly had a "*wanna*" or a "*gonna*" as if that validated his Americanness.

"Dad, can we go out to eat?" T.J. asked after he'd glanced at her.

She stopped her chopping to hear Tomide's response. T.J. had figured out his father was usually in a better mood when Jordan was around.

Tomide nodded. "Sure. What do you guys say to some burgers?"

The boys bounced excitedly on their seats. "Yes, please!"

Titilope packed up her chopped vegetables. She wouldn't mind a grilled chicken burger.

***

"Dad, I'm up!"

The cheerful voice yanked Titilope out of a vivid dream. She groaned as she opened her eyes. During Jordan's weekend visits their days began when he got up. He knocked on their door at about 6:30 a.m. while his brother could sleep until noon.

She tapped Tomide's shoulder. "Jordan needs his breakfast smoothie."

Tomide grunted as he pulled the blanket over his head. "Can't you see I'm still asleep?"

"Sleeping people don't talk."

"You've never heard of sleep talkers?"

Titilope pulled the blanket back down. She had stayed up late so that the boys could finish a movie. "Please, get up."

"Go and attend to him."

The muffled words made her blood rise. "Tomide."

He turned his back.

She counted down under her breath. "Five, four, three . . ."

"Aunty Titilope!"

Jaw clenched, she dragged herself up from the bed.

Jordan's eyes were bright when she opened their bedroom door. "Morning, Aunty," he greeted her with a big smile.

Titilope sighed. She could not stay angry with him. "Morning, Jordan."

Jordan laughed as he raced her downstairs. Titilope yawned as she opened the fridge to get the fruit for his smoothie. She surveyed her fruit options and picked up the container of strawberries. She would make him a strawberry-banana smoothie.

Jordan didn't like the new combination. "It doesn't taste the same," he said.

"I know. I had to use strawberries. We can get some raspberries from the store later."

Jordan held out the cup. "I don't want it."

Titilope took a calming breath. She placed a hand on his shoulder. "Remember, we talked about you trying different foods while you're here? Take another sip."

Jordan gave his head a vigorous shake. "No, thank you."

She collected the cup from him, dumped its contents in the sink and washed her hands. "I'm going back upstairs."

Jordan pushed out his lower lip. "But I'm still hungry. I want some scrambled eggs."

She lifted an eyebrow. "Excuse me?"

Jordan switched on his bright smile. "*Please.*"

Titilope shook her head. "That word is not going to work any magic this morning. I can toast some waffles, or you can wait until your dad gets up. Maybe he'll make the eggs."

Jordan glared at her before he spun around and headed towards the stairs. "Dad!"

Titilope crossed her arms and leaned against the kitchen island waiting for Tomide's appearance. He and Jordan entered the kitchen with matching scowls. "What's going on? Can't a man sleep after working hard all week?"

Certain Tomide wouldn't do anything stupid in Jordan's presence, she snorted. "We both went to work."

He took a step towards her. "You can't compare my job to yours."

Because she didn't work for the Federal Government, what she did wasn't important? "Jordan wants some eggs. Since you're awake, I'm sure you can make them for him."

"He told me you refused to make them?"

"That's right," she said.

Tomide's right hand moved so fast she didn't see it coming. The slap landed on the side of her face and temporarily blinded her left eye.

Stunned, she turned to Jordan and watched as a wet spot formed at the crotch of his Buzz Lightyear pyjama bottoms. "I want my mum!"

She held out a hand. "Jordan…"

He ran out of the room.

"You see what you've caused?" Tomide said before dashing after Jordan.

Titilope held a palm against her face. What had she done?

Even though Tomide apologised to her in front of Jordan, the boy sobbed until Tomide called his mother.

***

Holly took Jordan to the car before she spoke to Tomide. "Listen, I'm not going to put him through this again. Until you get your act together, Jordan will stay home."

Tomide glared at her. "You can't keep him away from me. He's my son too."

"Unfortunately," Holly said.

Titilope wrung her hands. T.J. would suffer from Jordan's absence. "Holly, I'm sorry. Everything was my fault," Titilope said.

"See, I told you," Tomide said.

Holly shook her head. "Titilope did nothing wrong."

Titilope sighed as Holly walked out of the house. She should have made the eggs.

CHAPTER FIVE

Tomide paced the bedroom floor with clenched fists. The terror on Jordan's face had shamed him. Regardless of how he felt about their mothers, he loved his sons. And even though he would never admit it, he loved Jordan just a little more because he looked like him.

He placed both fists on his head. He hadn't planned for things to escalate the way they had. Titilope was right. Everything is her fault. She had a way of getting under his skin.

Early on in their marriage, it became evident that Titilope didn't need or respect him the way he deserved. Even when he was forced to hit her, she would just stand there and take it as if he was nothing.

He glanced at the phone. Holly and Jordan should have arrived at their place. Because their divorce order said his visits with Jordan were at her discretion, Holly wielded the stipulation over his head like a sword. Tomide grimaced. He would have to keep apologising until she changed her mind.

When he felt calm enough to deal with Holly's attitude, he dialled her number.

She picked up after the fourth ring. "Titilope?"

"No, it's me."

"Right now, I don't feel like talking to you," she said.

Trust me the feeling is mutual. "I needed to tell you how sorry I am. It won't happen again."

Holly snickered. "You're talking to me, remember? I know you told everyone our marriage ended because I don't know how to take care of a man. That's bull. Tommy, you're outof control."

Her words were not helping him stay calm. "I guess I should have made the eggs for Jordan."

"You still don't get it. This incident is not about eggs. Titilope is not Jordan's slave. He sees how you treat her and probably thought it was okay for him to make demands of her. After our conversation, he knows better."

He stopped his pacing. "What happens between Titilope and me is none of your business."

"Jordan's exposure to your abusive behaviour concerns me."

Holly's frosty tone made his teeth clench. He took a deep breath. "Are you going to let him come back?"

"Tommy, you need help. Your sons are watching."

While they were married, Holly had bugged him about attending couples counselling. He had refused.

Since the counsellor could not teach her how to cook a decent African dish, what was the point?

He still wasn't interested in sitting on anyone's couch to unburden his soul. Some things need to stay buried. "Are you saying I have to attend counselling before Jordan can come back?"

Holly sighed. "No. It would be wasted on you since you're not ready to change."

"In that case, can he come back?"

All he heard was silence.

"Please, Holly."

"Fine."

He did a victory fist pump. Yes!

"For the record, I'm not doing this for you. It'd be unfair to punish the boys for your behaviour."

He remembered the planned travelling zoo visit. "So, can I pick up Jordan this afternoon? T.J. wants to spend time with him."

He heard Holly suck in air through her teeth. "You can pick him up."

Tomide smiled. "Thank you."

Holly disconnected the call.

***

T.J. gave him a puzzled look after he walked into Jordan's bedroom and found it empty. "Dad, I can't find Jordan. I even looked under his bed."

"Jordan went home," he said.

T.J.'s face fell. "Why?"

"His mum needed him. But we're going to pick him up later."

The transformation on T.J.'s face was instant. "Thanks, Dad."

"You're welcome. Go take a shower. I'll tell your mum you're up."

T.J. skipped out of the room.

Tomide went downstairs. Titilope sat, chin-in-hand, by the living room bay window. He stood in front of her. "I spoke to Holly."

She looked at him expectantly. "And?"

"I'm picking up Jordan, and we're going to the mall."

The distress on her face vanished. "Thank you."

Holly's annoying voice replayed in his ear. "I didn't do it for you."

She pulled herself up from the chair. "I'm sure T.J. needs my help."

As he watched her walk away, Tomide sighed. He wouldn't admit it to anyone, but, Holly was right. He had to make things right with the boys.

***

Tomide had never seen two children so happy to play with snakes. Nobody could pay him enough money to touch the reptiles.

When the boys announced their hunger, they went in search of the food truck. The bliss on their faces as they ate their hot dogs melted away some of Tomide's guilt.

He did struggle with managing his anger, but he was better than his father. Years earlier, when he had to write his father's eulogy, he could only draw from the two happy childhood memories. When he began sobbing, everyone thought it was due to grief.

Tomide cleared his throat. "Boys, from now on, we're going to have regular talks about man rules."

T.J. and Jordan exchanged a look.

"Why do we need to learn the rules? We're not yet men," Jordan said.

The boy had inherited his mother's sharp mouth. "The earlier you learn the lessons, the more time you'll have to work on them," he said.

"What's the number one rule?" T.J. asked.

Tomide cleared his throat. He was yet to plan the format for their talks. His mind went back to the morning's incident. "A man owns his mistakes."

He smiled at their blank expressions. "It's an adult way of saying, a man should admit when he's wrong and say sorry."

"Mum told me sorry means you won't do it again," T.J. said in a small voice.

He held T.J.'s eyes with his. "Sometimes, because we're human, we keep making the same mistakes."

T.J. cocked his head to the side. "Like the big mistakes you make?"

Tomide hadn't expected their man talks to start on a hard note. "Yes, like the big mistakes I make."

T.J. was silent for a few minutes. "Do girls have woman talks too?" he asked.

"I think that's where the mums tell them not to eat boogers," Jordan said with a knowledgeable air.

T.J.'s eyes widened. "Aha."

Tomide laughed. "What do you guys want to do next?"

"Donkey rides!" they said in unison.

He stood up. "Donkey ride, it is."

CHAPTER SIX

A glance at his watch confirmed they were late for the birthday party Kazeem organised for his wife. Tomide didn't believe in operating on Nigerian time. It was either he was punctual for events or stayed home.

Tomide raised his voice. "Woman, the party will be over before we get there," he said.

"I said I'm coming!" Titilope yelled from upstairs.

The irritated tone made Tomide purse his lips. He gave his watch a second look. If they were not down in fifteen minutes, he would leave without them.

Titilope and T.J. made it with three minutes to spare.

The party venue, a school gymnasium, was full. Bunmi waved Titilope and T.J. over to her table.

After he had wished Kazeem's wife a happy birthday, Tomide joined the men who were huddled together on the other side of the hall.

"Mr. Punctuality. I was wondering what had happened to you," Kazeem said.

"You know how these women like to waste time. Please, *chop knuckle*." Tomide gave Kazeem a fist bump. "This is fantastic."

"Thank you, friend," Kazeem said.

Tomide took the chair next to James. "My guy, how now?"

James grinned. "I *dey*. I was about to call your cell phone."

"I'm here now. Let the fun begin."

James hissed. "*Yeye* man. We were doing fine without you."

As the party got into full swing, another friend, Godspower, joined their table. He brought a stranger with him. "Guys, this is Eustace. He's visiting from Nigeria."

After the round of handshakes, the men sat back down. Tomide noticed the barely disguised disdain on Eustace's face as he scanned the venue.

Eustace turned to Godspower. "Bros, it's good you guys can get away with these low-budget parties. In Naija, if your party's not happening at an exclusive venue, preferably with a helipad, and you're not popping endless champagne bottles, no one with class is going to attend."

Around the table, the men dropped their forks.

As soon as Eustace left to get his food, Godspower gave Kazeem an apologetic look. "My guy, please don't mind the fool. He's my wife's younger cousin."

Kazeem waved away the apology. "We all have an idiot in-law like him."

Godspower snickered. "When the politician he launders money for loses the bid for re-election and he can't deliver mega deposits for his bank, Eustace will be popping bottles of cheap *ogogoro* with his new zero class friends."

They were still laughing when Eustace returned with a full plate.

Big Boy Eustace didn't have a problem with low-budget party food, Tomide thought as he chewed on his fried chicken. What a jerk.

Tomide was in the middle of a conversation with James when Eustace called his name.

"I think I know you from somewhere," Eustace said when Tomide glanced his way.

Eustace wasn't the type of man he wanted to know. "I don't think so."

"I know you. How can you forget this face? We owned Lafenwa."

Lafenwa was his old neighbourhood in Abeokuta. Tomide took a second look at Eustace. Wow. He should have recognised the beady eyes. Back in the day, Eustace was known as *Omo Olowo Adugbo* alias *Khashoggi Jr.* Their family had oppressed the entire neighbourhood with roaring diesel generators and Alsatian dogs.

Tomide snickered. It made sense that Khashoggi Jr. had grown into an obnoxious man. As a child, he'd been a first-class bully. "You changed your name," he said.

"Yeah. Eustace is classier than Aina."

While Tomide thought of a politically correct response, James, who looked like he'd been trying to stifle a laugh, choked on his drink.

Tomide patted his friend on the back. "I never imagined that we'd meet again," he said to Eustace.

"Me too. Who would have thought Mighty Igor's son and I would sit at the same table? Living abroad is a leveller."

Eustace's face swam before Tomide's eyes. Hearing his father's nickname had brought unwanted memories. On the days when his father locked the doors to deal with his mother's sharp tongue, the whole neighbourhood had front row seats to their shameful show. Tomide's chest rose and fell in rapidly. He'd worked so hard to leave the slurs from the past behind him. He was more than Mighty Igor's son.

As the room spun in different shades of red, Tomide sprang from his seat. The sudden movement rattled the folding table and toppled the plate of hot pounded yam and *egusi* soup into Eustace's crotch.

"What is this nonsense?" Eustace yelled as he jumped to his feet.

Tomide felt a gentle hand on his arm. It was James.

"Bro, let's go outside and get some fresh air."

Tomide shook away James' hand. "I have to go. Sorry, Kazeem." He marched in Titilope's direction.

Behind him, Tomide heard Godspower's loud voice. "*Onisokuso*. Why couldn't you keep your leaky mouth shut?"

***

T.J. saw him coming. He left his friends and hurried towards his mother. Tomide narrowed his eyes. Why did the child always act as if he was a monster?

T.J. tugged on his mother's blouse sleeve and Titilope looked in his direction. He pointed towards the door. Titilope stood up and gathered her things.

Titilope was ready by the time he reached her side. He gave Kazeem's wife an apologetic smile. "Sorry, we have to leave. T.J. had a fever in the morning. It's best he has an early night."

"I'm glad you guys still came," she said. "It means a lot to us."

T.J. gave his mother a puzzled look. "But I didn't—"

Tomide stepped forward. "T.J., let's go. Mum will meet us in the car."

During the drive home, Tomide clenched the steering wheel as he floored the accelerator. Several times, he took his foot off and slammed on the brakes, bringing the car to a complete stop. The adrenaline rush made him feel better.

They were almost at the house when Titilope spoke to him. "Did I do something wrong?"

He kept his eyes on the road as he snapped the words. "Not everything is about you."

After he'd parked the car, she and T.J. hurried inside the house. By the time he came upstairs, Titilope had locked herself in the bathroom. Tomide scratched his head at the retching sounds. He'd forgotten that she was prone to motion sickness. He knocked on the door. "There's some nausea medication downstairs. I can bring you some."

Titilope didn't respond.

He knocked again. "Are you okay?"

Titilope ignored him. He mumbled an apology and left the room. It wasn't about her. He'd just wanted to silence Khashoggi Jr.'s voice in his head.

CHAPTER SEVEN

The server placed their food on the table. "I forget to tell you that we offer six-dollar mojitos and margaritas on Thursdays," she said.

Tomide gave an exaggerated sigh. "That offer sounds great. But, we have to go back to work."

She smiled as she picked up her tray. "Enjoy your meal."

"We have something important to discuss," James said after she left.

Tomide shifted in his seat. He'd known James had something on his mind when he'd insisted on a lunch date. "What is it?"

Even though no one sat close, James lowered his voice. "We've been friends far too long for me to hear these troubling reports and keep them to myself."

Titilope must have opened her mouth to James' busybody wife. He took a bite from his turkey sandwich before he spoke. "What did you hear?"

"I heard, from several sources, that you've been beating up Titilope," James said.

Tomide shook his head. "After thirty years of friendship, you still need to ask me such a question?"

Sweat beads formed on James' brow. "Tomide—"

"Man, I'm disappointed. You should be the one shutting down any rumour."

James leaned forward. "And I've been doing exactly that."

"Then why are you asking me this question?"

"I thought you might need me to help you figure things out."

His appetite ruined, Tomide pushed away his plate. While he was in his crusader mode, James was more persistent than an addict in search of a fix. He had to give him something.

"You have to promise to keep what I'm about to tell you between the two of us. If you must tell your wife, this is the time to let me know."

James' tone was clipped. "I don't tell Bunmi everything we talk about."

He offered James a placating half-smile. "*No vex*. Saying these words is hard for me."

"Bro, what is going on?"

Tomide ran a hand over his bald head. "The truth is Titilope has been physically abusing me."

James' expression swung between shock and disbelief. "Your wife has been physically abusing you? Is this a joke?"

"Does it sound like something any man will joke about?"

James blinked several times. "But how is it possible? Titilope's much smaller than you. And how does that explain the scars and wounds on her body?"

Interesting. So Titilope had graduated from shooting off her mouth to showing off her body. He threw up his hands. "Forget I said anything. I guess you're one of those deluded people who believe women can't abuse men."

"Tomide, calm down. I had to ask the question."

He spat the words out through clenched teeth. "Women can be abusive. Physical strength has nothing to do with it."

James drew out his sigh. "What happened?"

"I'm sure you remember how things went down with Holly." Since the smoothie incident, saying Holly's name left a bitter taste in his mouth.

He mimicked Holly's high-pitched Californian drawl. "Tommy, fix this. Tommy, clean that. Tommy, you need to learn how to cook. Tommy, please bend over and let me kick your behind."

"I didn't know things were that bad," James said.

He leaned against the table. "Oh, yes they were. God saved me from that woman. Her real plan was to emasculate me. The only thing she didn't ask me to do was wash her dirty panties."

James shuddered. "Nasty business."

"You can say that again. With Titilope, I thought things would be different. She's one of us. But, before I knew it, she'd written me a chore list and made herself the housework patrol cop. Something my mother with her double Master's degrees wouldn't have tried. Can you imagine her asking my father to cook for her?"

"From what I remember of him, that would have been an act of war," James said.

His father had ruled his home with two iron fists. "No real man will stand by and let that liberated 'I-am-woman-hear–me-roar' nonsense take control of his woman."

James nodded his agreement. "Before Bunmi opens her mouth to say, 'I am woman,' she'll be dragging bags through her parents' door."

The words brought a wan smile to Tomide's face. Perhaps he'd overestimated Bunmi's hold on his friend.

James cleared his throat. "On a serious note, Bunmi and I have come a long way. Things are better when couples compromise."

His blood boiled at James' self-depreciating smile. Bunmi had ruined his friend.

"I know you live with Titilope. Still, it all sounds so out of character," James said.

"We did okay for maybe…the first two years. Things changed after T.J.'s arrival. When I refused to become a houseboy in my home, Titilope snapped. The first time it happened, she threw a kitchen knife at me."

James blinked. "Titilope tried to stab you?"

"My experience from dodging my father's blows saved me," he said.

James looked confused. "This doesn't make sense."

"Those marks you talked about?"

"What about them?" James asked.

Tomide took his time as he unbuttoned his sleeves and rolled them up to expose a mix of healed and new scars along the length of both arms. "Titilope mutilates herself when she's angry. She does this to me when I try to make her stop."

Wide-eyed, James sank in his seat. "Oh my God."

He drew out a heavy sigh. "After what happened to my mother, do you think I'd put my hands on a woman, no matter the provocation?"

James looked shamefaced. "I'm sorry. Maybe it's best you leave her before she kills you."

"I know the danger. But, I'm staying for my son's sake. Despite her behaviour towards me, Titilope loves T.J. And at his age, T.J. needs his mother."

James sighed. "You're in a damned-if-you-do, damned-if-you-don't situation."

He rolled down his sleeves. "Yes, I am."

James glanced at his watch. "I need to head back to work."

He stood and gave James a quick hug. "Thanks, man. I know you're watching out for me."

James patted him on the back. "Anytime. I'm glad we had this talk."

James now had something to tell the busybodies. "Me too."

Tomide's stomach growled during his walk back to the office. Thanks to Titilope's loose lips, he'd wasted a tasty lunch.

A tingling sensation went through his body. He will leave work early. Titilope needed a reminder of their number one house rule: no talking to outsiders about what happens in their home.

CHAPTER EIGHT

"Dad's home," T.J. said in a sombre voice. He had been singing along with the radio.

Titilope parked the mini-van by the curb. "Yes, he is," she said with forced cheer.

The sight of Tomide's car had quickened her pulse. With the Washington D.C. rush hour traffic, he usually didn't make it back to their Rockville home before 6.00 p.m. She gave herself a mental kick for not putting T.J.'s swimming things in the car when she'd thought about them in the morning.

Titilope stepped out of the car and waited for T.J. to unbuckle his seat belt. With luck on their side, Tomide would be in his basement man cave, and they could sneak in and out of the house without catching his attention.

She paused at the bottom of their front steps and gave T.J. a warning. "You have to be quiet. We'll go straight up to your room, get your things and leave."

"Okay, Mum," T.J. whispered.

Her heart jumped when she pushed open the front door and saw Tomide pacing the foyer. "Hello."

"I heard you've been conducting show-and-tell sessions around town," Tomide said.

His words didn't make sense. Titilope's eyes darted to her son's anxious face. *No swimming lessons tonight*, she thought as she reached for his hand. She'd been at the receiving end of Tomide's anger far too many times not to recognise the promise reflected in his flinty eyes.

She gave him a weak smile. "Please, let me take T.J. up to his room. We'll talk about this when I get back."

"T.J.'s almost five, not a baby. He's capable of getting himself upstairs."

She held on to T.J.'s hand as they backed away from him. "It will only take a couple of minutes."

Tomide tipped his head in the direction of the stairs. They both ran up. She closed T.J.'s bedroom door behind them and leaned against it. "Please, change into your pyjamas."

T.J shook his head. "I want to go swimming. We have our swim test today."

She knew how much he wanted to move on to the next level. "Sweetie, I'm sorry. You'll take your test on another day."

Tears filled his eyes. "I've been practicing. It's not fair!"

Titilope sighed. It wasn't. "*Pele*." It was one of the few Yoruba words T.J. knew.

T.J. stomped his feet. "You keep saying sorry. And I haven't had any dinner!"

She fought back her tears. "Please, don't raise your voice at me. You can have a little snack now. I'll bring dinner later."

T.J.'s shoulders slumped. "I'm sorry for yelling, Mum. Will you forgive me?"

"Of course." She gave him a quick hug before she opened his closet door. Thank God she'd remembered to fill his emergency snack bin. She handed T.J. a juice box and a bag of baked pita chips.

T.J.'s chin quivered as he held on to the snacks. "Do you have to go?"

It was best to get downstairs before Tomide came looking for her. In an agitated state, he was unpredictable. "Yes, sweetie. I have to."

She found T.J.'s audio CD of *How to Train Your Dragon* and inserted it in the boom box.

After she had made him sit on his bed, she increased the volume. "Do you remember what I said about not coming out of your room until I say it's okay to do so?"

He nodded. "Uh-huh."

She gave him another hug. "I'll be back soon."

"Promise?"

Titilope nodded.

She closed the door behind her and leaned against it for a couple of moments before she took measured steps down the stairs.

When Tomide saw her, he began to whistle. The upbeat tune made Titilope tremble. Her eyes followed Tomide as he walked around the living room and closed the blinds.

Titilope ran the morning's events through her mind. There were no arguments, no forgotten tasks. She'd done nothing to incur his wrath.

Tomide paced in front of the knife block for a few seconds before he opened the fridge and brought out a bottle of water. The water sloshed as he poured some into a glass cup. "Why did you tell Bunmi I was beating you?"

Her denial was swift. "I did not tell Bunmi anything."

She flinched when Tomide pounded a fist on the counter. "Stop pretending!"

Titilope stepped closer to him. With the right words, T.J. might still make his swimming class. "I swear on my life. I didn't tell Bunmi anything. Last month, she saw some bruises when we took the boys for a swim. I told her I'd slipped on a slick sidewalk. I guess she didn't believe me."

Tomide snickered. "Liar. You wore a bathing suit because you wanted Bunmi to see your body."

She'd forgotten about the bruises. "I couldn't swim in my clothes."

When her fingertips grazed his skin, Tomide swung his arm back. His fist landed on the side of her head. "How dare you touch me?"

Her head crashed into the kitchen cabinet. The glass door shattered. Titilope whimpered as a shard pierced her cheek before it landed on the floor. "I didn't do anything wrong."

"Do you realise what you've done to me? I've become a laughingstock."

She cowered as Tomide moved toward her. "I'm sorry."

"You just said you didn't do anything wrong. What are you sorry for?"

The second blow across the face knocked her to the ground. Her hands flew over her head as she tried to deflect a kick. "I lied. Yes, I had wanted Bunmi to see the scars."

Tomide shook his head. "Why do you keep telling these lies?"

She'd learned the beatings ended much sooner if she said what he wanted to hear or didn't fight him. "It won't happen again."

"You'd better pray this is the last I hear of this nonsense." Tomide stepped over her as he walked out of the room.

Sprawled on the cold ceramic tiles, blood from the cut on her face pooled beside her head. Titilope closed her eyes as her mind travelled back to childhood days in Nigeria.

It was dark outside. Brow furrowed, her younger self, stood by her open bedroom window with shaky hands placed against the mosquito net screen. Their neighbour, Mummy Maria was screaming. "Daddy

Maria, please, it's enough. The wounds from last week are yet to heal."

Desperate, Titilope went to her mother. Mummy had listened to her concerns and given two directives. "Lock your bedroom windows. Pull your curtains shut."

She had wanted to do more. "Mummy Maria needs to leave that man."

"Leave? A good mother does not run from her child's home. She always stays, and she fights."

From what Titilope could hear, Mummy Maria was on the losing side. "Is there nothing we can do for her?"

Mummy had given her a warning look. "We don't interfere between a man and his wife. Such fights are a family affair. With time, they will settle their problems. Then you, the peacemaker, will become their common enemy."

As directed, Titilope had kept her windows closed. Life moved on.

"Mum. Mum, where are you? You said you would be back soon. Mum!"

The sound of T.J.'s trembling voice brought more pain than Tomide's fist had caused. She couldn't let him see her in a bloodied state. He already had night terrors. Her body shook from muffled cries as T.J. continued to call for her.

CHAPTER NINE

Titilope stood in the middle of her vanilla scented kitchen and wiped a film of wheat flour off her face. Every inch of her granite countertop had rows of blueberry and banana muffins, ten dozen in all. She had yet to figure out the connection between pain and her need to bake.

She dragged herself to the kitchen sink and began to wash up. She had called her office and told her supervisor she was sick because the concealer had failed to cover her bruises.

In six months, she'd missed twenty-eight workdays. Titilope knew it was only a matter of time before she was called down to HR.

Titilope dried her hands and sat down to catch her breath. Her freezer still had several bags of muffins. She decided to send some packages to Bunmi and Holly. Since Tomide was in a contrite mood, he would deliver them.

Through the open blinds, Titilope saw the delivery man throw a bundle of shopping flyers at her door. She stood up and headed outside to pick it up. Her hand was on the door handle when Holly arrived. She took one look at Titilope's face and gasped. "What happened to you?"

A cry of pain escaped when she tried to smile. "I fell when I was running down the stairs at work."

Holly followed her into the house. "It must have been a bad fall."

She tightened her housecoat sash. "It looks worse than it feels."

"I was wondering why you were home when Tomide said I could stop by to pick up Jordan's skateboard." Holly sniffed the air. "What is that yummy smell?"

"I've been baking," she said.

Holly's eyes widened when she saw the muffins. "You're starting a baked goods business?"

"No. I just had too much energy. Would you like to sample one?"

Holly pulled out a kitchen chair. "No, thanks. I have something I need to show you." Holly pulled some papers out of her tote and held them out. "T.J. drew these during his last visit."

Titilope's hands shook as she took the papers. There were two drawings of stick figures labelled "Mum and Dad." Stick Figure Mum was on the floor while Stick Figure Dad loomed over her. In one drawing, large red teardrops trailed from Stick Figure Mum's face and pooled around her. The words "bad dad" were written on the papers. The third drawing was a little stick figure lying in bed. The large eyes and an upside-down smile painted a picture of sadness.

The words were out before she could stop herself. "T.J. doesn't see anything."

Holly sighed. "He hears everything."

Titilope scrunched up the papers. And she'd thought she was doing a good job of protecting her child. Tomide was right. She was a total failure.

"Since the smoothie incident, I've struggled with sending Jordan here for visits. Every time, I ask myself, what is he learning? I can go back to court to get Tommy's access changed. But how do I tell my child cancelling their visits is my way of protecting him from the father he adores?"

Tomide wouldn't harm his golden child. "Jordan's safe," she said.

"What about your son?"

Red-hot shame made her jump to Tomide's defense. "Right now, Tomide's going through a difficult time. The pressure of work. Money issues. He doesn't handle stress well."

Holly shook her head. "Many men struggle with those same issues. They don't batter their wives."

"Your marriage to him was different," she said.

Holly went pale. "I've never told anyone this. Tomide also hit me. Twice. I decided not to wait around for the third time."

Titilope's jaw dropped. Tomide told her that he had ended the marriage. That guilt made him give Holly a lot of control around his visits with Jordan. "I'm sorry."

Holly dropped her gaze. "You've done nothing wrong. I owe you an overdue apology. The first day we met, I was rude. While we were together, Tomide kept telling me I should have known what I was getting myself into when I married a conservative African man. He made me feel like I was somewhat deficient."

"Tomide is an expert at projecting his feelings of deficiency on others." The knowledge didn't make his hurtful words easier to live with.

Holly nodded. "When he told me he'd found an appropriate wife, someone who'd agreed to his so-called terms, I'd felt that your acceptance made you unworthy of my respect. I'm sorry."

Tomide always said that she had changed. But there had been no serious conversation around his expectations.

"Apology accepted. For the record, our women are not pathetic like me. And not all our men are abusive like Tomide."

Holly frowned. "I'm not going to condemn an entire country because of one person's actions. And please, don't call yourself that word."

Titilope glanced at the ball of papers in her hand. She was pathetic. "Thank you for bringing these."

Holly's blue eyes were dark with worry. "You have to do something about this. If Tommy doesn't get the help he needs, one day, he's going to kill you. Titilope, he's going to kill you."

***

Titilope waited until T.J. had finished his afterschool snack before she brought up Holly's visit. She placed the smoothed-out papers on the kitchen table. "Sweetie, did you draw these?"

With widened eyes, T.J. nodded.

"Aunty Holly said you hear noises from your room?"

"Yeah."

"Why didn't you tell me?"

T.J. looked confused. "Because you said mums know everything."

Titilope left her seat and knelt before T.J.'s chair. "We're going to be fine. I promise."

T.J. gave her a solemn look. "Pinky promise?"

Titilope stuck out her little finger and T.J. curved his around it.

"Pinky promise."

CHAPTER TEN

Titilope glanced at her vibrating cell phone. Tomide's number flashed across the screen. Why wouldn't he leave her alone?

After she'd spent an hour dealing with T.J.'s early morning tantrum about how he was never going to get promoted to the otter swim group because he'd missed his swimming test, she had little energy or patience for Tomide's romantic "the days after" charade.

As much as she'd wanted to scream at T.J., she knew they were both trying to cope the best way they could.

T.J. calmed down after she bribed him with a movie and fast food night. With the way things were going, she was going to be one of the contenders for the Bad Parent of the Year Award. Titilope switched off her cell phone.

When Tomide began calling her work number, she ignored the ringing phone.

"Titilope, are you there?" one of her pod mates asked. There was a tinge of annoyance in her voice.

"Yes," she said.

"Please, get your phone. I'm trying to finish a report and I can't think with that noise."

"Sorry." She lifted the receiver. "Hello?"

"There you are, *wifey*. How's your day going?"

At the sound of Tomide's cheery voice, her migraine upgraded itself from mild to pounding. "What do you want?"

"No hello for me? Well, I want to take you out for lunch," he said.

Eating was the last thing on her mind. "I have to leave the office for an appointment."

Tomide gave a little laugh. "Really?"

The half-truth rolled off her lips. "Yes. I need to drop off a report at a client's office."

"Your receptionist told me your schedule was clear until later in the day," he said.

Titilope frowned. "My receptionist?"

"Yes. Ms. Darlene. I'm in your office lobby."

Titilope rubbed circles on her left temple. "We just rescheduled," she said.

"Since it's your lunch hour, I'm sure it can wait. I already made reservations."

T.J. didn't need another chaotic night. "I'll be out soon."

She made a quick detour to the bathroom and splashed some water on her face.

When he saw her, Tomide ended his conversation with Darlene. He walked over and gave her a hug. "Is this top new? The colour suits you."

Conscious of their attentive audience, she played along. "I used one of the gift cards you got me."

"There's more where that came from," Tomide said with a wink.

On their way out, Darlene gave her the thumbs up sign. "Enjoy your lunch."

"Oh, she will," Tomide said before Titilope could respond. "She always does."

***

"Why are you wasting your food?" Tomide asked when she dropped her fork and pushed aside her plate.

The punch to her jaw made chewing difficult. "It's not soft enough."

"Then you should have sent it back to the kitchen." Tomide forked a piece of his poached fish and held it out. "This is delicious."

"No, thank you."

Tomide scowled when she refused the offer a second time. "I'm just trying to make sure you have a good time."

Titilope sighed. "You get an A for effort."

Tomide shifted in his seat and pulled out a little, blue box from his coat pocket. "This present will get

"Yes, dear. The police officers are on their way. I want you to stay on the telephone with me until the officers get there."

T.J. rubbed his eyes. He really wanted his mum. "Okay."

The telephone receiver fell from T.J.'s hand when he heard another loud scream from downstairs.

"Hello. Hello. T.J., are you still there?"

He stared at the telephone for a couple of minutes before he picked it up. "I have to go help Mum now."

"No, T.J. You have to stay where you are," the woman said in a firm voice.

The woman sounded mad. "I have to go. Thank you. Bye."

"Wait!"

T.J. clicked off the telephone.

me an A plus. Happy Birthday. I'm sure you thought I forgot."

She remembered when she had to date a report.

Tomide slid the Tiffany box across the table. "Open it."

She did, and her eyes widened at the sight of the diamond and ruby tennis bracelet. It was beautiful. But, the more she stared at the jewellery, the more each ruby stone looked like the drops of blood in T.J.'s drawing. "I can't accept this."

Tomide frowned. "Why not? It's more than my mother got."

When their marriage began to unravel, she had nurtured some resentment against her mother-in-law for raising such a man. During the woman's one and only visit to their home, she had discovered that Tomide had little regard for his mother despite her open adoration. Titilope's resentment had turned to pity.

"I don't need another bribe," she said.

He gave her a shaky smile. "About the other night. With all the stress at work and dealing with Holly's shenanigans, my temper has been a little short. It won't happen again. I promise."

Titilope wondered how he could sound so sincere. "Tomide, you…we…need to get some help."

Tomide sat back in his seat and crossed his arms. "I guess I have Holly to thank for that suggestion?"

"This isn't about Holly."

Tomide snorted. "We both know it is."

She shook her head. "This is about me. Tomide, I'm drowning. I don't know how much longer I have."

Tomide began tapping his fingers on the table. "Did I ever tell you about the near-drowning experience I had when I was nine?"

There'd been too many stories. "I'm not sure."

Tomide had his eyes on her, but she could tell his mind was somewhere else. "It was horrible. I'd gone to the beach with an older cousin. Because he was busy flirting, he didn't notice when I went into the water. A huge wave crashed over me. It dragged me under and pulled me further out to sea. With each gasp, my lungs filled with water. I began to sink."

Titilope was shocked when his eyes filled with tears. She'd never seen him cry.

"Those minutes before help came felt like an eternity. I was sure I was going to die."

The sight of Tomide's tears made Titilope feel brave. She leaned over the table and whispered her words.

"When you wrap your hands around my throat, what you described is how I feel."

Tomide's chest expanded as he inhaled. "I try. But, I can't help myself. The anger overpowers me."

"That's why we need help."

"We can handle this ourselves. We don't need an outsider to tell us how to live our lives."

Titilope shook her head. "We can't do this on our own."

"I'll have to think about this."

The set jaw told Titilope she'd pushed him enough. "Whatever you say."

Tomide reached for the box and took out the bracelet. "Are you going to wear it?"

She held out her arm, and he fastened the bracelet around her wrist. "I knew it would be perfect for you," he said with a pleased smile.

Titilope stared at the glistening jewels. The diamonds were like teardrops. Her blood and tears in exchange for a trinket.

She knew that as soon as she arrived at the office, she would take off the bracelet and it would never touch her skin again.

CHAPTER ELEVEN

Titilope yawned as she wrapped herself in an oversized bathrobe. It was tax season, and after a long work week, she'd planned her Friday evening around two things, a relaxing bath and a good book.

She turned as the bedroom door opened. Tomide poked in his head. "The boys are hungry. Anything for us?"

"There are some bags of chips and salsa in the pantry," she offered.

Tomide shook his head. "I already promised them pepper soup. Hurry."

Which kain wahala be dis? Titilope pulled out some clothes from her closet.

She was halfway down the stairs when she stopped to assess the situation. First, the goat meat had to be defrosted, then chopped into small cubes. It would take at least an hour for her to prep and cook the dish. A lavender-scented bubble bath was a better choice.

Titilope squared her shoulders. One night of snacks would not make her a bad hostess. She turned around and headed back to their bedroom.

She was in the bath when Tomide came to look for her. "Titilope, what are you doing?"

"Relaxing," Titilope said as she wiggled her toes to the beat of the song playing on the shower radio.

"What?" The locked door handle jiggled.

Titilope smiled. She'd known he would barge into the room.

"Where's the pepper soup I asked for?" Tomide said.

"I didn't say I was going to cook anything."

"What did you just say?"

She could imagine the fumes coming out of his ears. "You heard me."

"Titilope, don't make me break down this door."

Her breath quickened as she waited for Tomide's next move. Instead of kicks, she heard footsteps and James' deep voice. "Tomide, *we dey go club o*. Are you coming?"

"Titilope, see what you've caused? I said, open this door!"

She had no intention of doing as he had asked.

James spoke again. "Tomide, it's no big deal. We'll eat at the club. Let's go."

Titilope closed her eyes when she heard their receding footsteps. Temporary bliss.

***

After her bath, Titilope took her novel and sat at the kitchen table. Alcohol had two effects on her husband. He was either going to come back from the club extremely agitated or super relaxed. With T.J. in bed, it was best to contain the fallout downstairs.

She must have dozed off because she opened her eyes and found Tomide standing over her. From the wild look in his eyes, she could tell it was an agitated kind of night.

"Titilope, what is your problem? What kind of woman embarrasses her husband by refusing to cook for his guests? I'm not sure if the problem is that your parents didn't train you or you were unable to learn."

She stretched out the kink in her side. "You can say whatever you want about me. Please, leave my parents out of this."

Tomide thumped his chest. "In case you forgot, this is my house. I'll damn well say anything I want about anyone."

Her teeth clenched. "Not about my parents."

Tomide moved close. "What did you say?"

The calm voice in her head told her to shut up. She ignored it. "I said, not about my parents."

Before she could catch the next breath, Tomide swung his hand back and hit her across the face. The chair flew back, and her head slammed into the refrigerator.

Glee was back in Tomide's eyes. "What else do you have to say?"

Titilope was silent as she staggered to her feet.

"I said what else do you have to say?"

Titilope wondered if she'd be able to get around him and run out through the front door.

"Oh, now you want to keep quiet? Too late. Today, you're going to answer my questions even if I have to break every bone in your body."

She backed away from him. Her breath came quickly, each subsequent one a little harder to take. As she fought a light-headed feeling, hysterical laughter welled up in her throat. When it spewed out of her mouth, they were both caught off guard by the robust sound.

Fist suspended in the air, Tomide gaped at her. "What's so funny?"

She wiped the blood from the corner of her mouth with the back of her hand. "You, Tomide Ojo. If only you know how bad your desperation for relevance stinks. Remember the stories you told me about leaving Holly? Holly left you."

Tomide's eyes bulged. "Holly is a liar."

She shook her head. "You're the one with no integrity. Some days, the sight of your face makes me sick."

Tomide lunged at her. "Shut up!"

She began to laugh. "Are my words affecting you? I guess the truth has sharp teeth."

"I said, shut up!"

Even after Tomide grabbed her by her braids and jerked her around the room like a rag doll, she couldn't stop laughing.

"Shut up! I said shut up!" As he said each word, Tomide slammed her head into the wall.

The voice in her head intensified its warning. *Titilope, stop it! Stop! He's going to kill you!*

Even after her laughter turned into gurgling sounds because of the pool of blood in her mouth, Titilope found she could no longer keep quiet.

***

Upstairs, T.J.'s body jerked several times as he listened to the noise. He was used to his father's loud, angry voice, the sound of glass breaking and furniture crashing. The difference was his mother's screams. Each high-pitched scream echoed inside his head. He began to cry.

As he dug fingers deep into his ears, T.J. remembered what his teacher at the day care, Ms. Paula, had told them. When anyone was hurt, they were to call 911 and help would come.

T.J. got out of bed and opened the door to his room. Because he'd been told not to leave his room, he fell to his knees and crawled across the landing. He needed a telephone, and there was one in the guest bedroom.

When he got there, T.J. took the phone and hid in the closet. He mouthed the numbers as he punched them in. Soon, he heard a woman's voice.

"911. What's your emergency?"

The woman's voice sounded kind. "My dad's hurting my mum," he said.

"Your dad's hurting your mum?" the woman asked.

T.J. clamped his thighs together at the sudden urge to pee. Dad wouldn't like it if he peed on himself like a baby. "Uh-huh."

"What is your name?"

"T.J."

"T.J., how old are you?" she asked.

He held up his fingers. "I'm four."

Because he was almost four and a half, he'd also bent his thumb. T.J. frowned. He wasn't sure if he needed to tell the woman about the half part.

"Okay T.J., where are you?"

He looked around. "I'm in the closet," he said.

"Is the closet at your home?"

"Uh-huh."

"Are you hurt?"

He shook his head.

"T.J.?"

It felt as if it something heavy was on his chest. But no one had placed anything there. "No."

He couldn't see it but could hear the woman's smile. "You've been a good boy," she said. "Where are your mum and dad?"

"They're downstairs. Are you going to send someone to help my mum?"

CHAPTER TWELVE

Titilope sat by the window. Through her open blinds, she saw curious neighbours standing outside their homes. It wasn't every day an ambulance and police cruisers spent hours on the quiet street.

She could make out the outline of Tomide's bowed head from where he sat at the back of the police cruiser. When he refused to leave, he was handcuffed and dragged out of the house.

T.J. sat next to her. His hold around her body was tight. She could barely breathe.

"Excuse me, ma'am."

Through swollen eyes, Titilope peered at the police officer in front of her. "Yes."

His tone was soft. "Whenever there's a child present during a domestic violence call, we have to notify CPS. A worker will be arriving shortly."

The words sent a chill through her. "Officer, Tomide has never laid a hand on my son. You can ask him. We don't need CPS."

"Ma'am, I'm just following our standard protocol." The officer walked away.

While she still lived in Nigeria, she'd heard about these child protection workers. Those who visited said the workers received bonuses each time they removed a child from the family home. If this person took T.J. away from her, the separation would finish her.

By the time the CPS worker walked into the house, Titilope was dizzy from her pain and fear.

"Hello. My name is Amy Gustav."

She was silent as the worker sat in the chair across from her.

Amy gave her a smile. "I understand you've had a rough evening. I'm here to help in any way I can."

More like here to help yourself to my son. Titilope rubbed T.J.'s head.

Amy spent the next fifteen minutes asking different questions and taking down notes. "If you don't mind, I'd like to have a private chat with T.J."

T.J. shook his head. "No."

Titilope tightened her arm around her son. "You don't need to interview him. Like I already told the officer, Tomide loves T.J. He doesn't hurt him."

"It will be a short interview," Amy said.

"As you can see, you're scaring him. Is that how you want to help us?"

Amy pursed her lips as she took down more notes.

It was hard, but Titilope read some of the upside-down text.

Immigrant family. Limited support system. The mother is assuming responsibility and making excuses for the father's actions.

Amy closed her notebook after she looked up and their eyes met. "Is there someone who can watch T.J. over the next couple of days? The paramedics are waiting to take you to the hospital. Given what happened, it'll be best if T.J. stays with people he's familiar with."

"You're not going to take him?"

"I'll have to bring him into the temporary care of the agency if you don't have somewhere safe for him to go," Amy said.

"You mean you'll put him in a stranger's home?"

"A safe foster home. Yes."

T.J. began to sob. "Please don't let her take me away. I'll be good. I promise."

"Sweetie, it's fine."

There were only two people she could call. She chose Bunmi. It would be unfair to Holly to put her in the middle of their mess. Until Jordan became an adult, she had to deal with Tomide.

T.J. continued to cry. If she had the power, she would erase the memory of what he'd heard and seen that night. But she didn't.

"Do you need me to get the phone for you?" Amy asked.

Titilope wiped her son's face. She pulled herself up. "No, thank you."

***

Titilope made her call in the kitchen. Bunmi answered the phone. "*Ore*, I need your help."

"Titilope?" Bunmi asked.

The pain in her jaw had affected her speech. "Yes."

Bunmi's voice became alarmed. "Are you okay?"

"No. I need you to take T.J. for a couple of days. CPS is here."

She heard Bunmi's sharp intake of air. "James will come and get him. Don't worry, he'll be safe with us."

When she returned to the living room, Amy requested a quick meeting in the foyer. "How did your conversation go?"

"My friend's husband is on his way."

"Good. Please pack some of T.J.'s favourite toys, so he'll have something familiar with him at your friend's place. You'll also need to assure him that you'll get better. Do you think you can talk to him without my assistance?"

I've been taking care of him before you showed up. "Yes."

T.J. wailed when she told him he couldn't go with her to the hospital. "You're not coming back."

Titilope fought her tears. "That's not true. You're going to Aunty Bunmi's house. Your friends are there. Tomorrow, Aunty Bunmi will bring you to the hospital for a visit."

T.J. narrowed his eyes. "She won't forget?"

"I'll call to remind her."

As she walked upstairs to pack T.J.'s bag, Amy struck a conversation with him. Titilope was sure the worker would sneak in some of her questions.

With each outfit and toy she placed inside the duffle bag, Titilope's chest tightened. What if T.J. never came back home?

She sat on his bed, leaned over the bag and stuffed a hand into her mouth. She couldn't afford to let Amy hear her cry. She'd only write more things in her damning notepad. Titilope could picture the small, neat script. *Mother emotionally unstable. Unfit to be a parent.*

The doorbell rang, and she heard Amy call out her name from downstairs. "Titilope, James is here."

She wiped her face with one of T.J.'s dirty shirts and picked up Mr. Bear, T.J.'s ragged plush toy, from his bed. The old toy should give him some comfort.

Downstairs, James took a step back when he saw her. "*Jesu.* Titilope, what happened?"

"We'll talk later. Please, tell Bunmi I'll call her in the morning."

T.J. was half-asleep when James carried him out of the house. It had been a long day.

After they had left, she turned to Amy. "There. I've sent my child away. Happy?"

Amy placed a hand on her arm. "It's time for you to go to the hospital. You need to get well for your son. He needs you."

Titilope moved away. She didn't want anybody's touch. "T.J. needs me."

Amy nodded. "Yes, he does."

Titilope dragged herself across the room and picked up her purse and keys from the kitchen table. Amy walked out, and she locked the door behind them.

CHAPTER THIRTEEN

Shoulders hunched, legs wedged against the steep plating behind the front seat, Tomide squirmed in the back of the police cruiser. He couldn't find a comfortable position. He grimaced as he tried hard to ignore a back itch. There was no way he could attend to it with handcuffed hands.

An officer had read his Miranda rights, but he still hoped that Titilope would ask the officers to let him go. He'd had wanted to apologise to her, but the officers had dragged him outside.

A young woman he didn't recognise walked up to their townhouse. One of the officers opened the door for her. A short while later, the officers came outside. Tomide tried to sit up when he saw them walking toward the cruiser. When the officers got into the vehicle without saying anything to him, Tomide knew he was in big trouble.

By the time they arrived at the Montgomery County Detention Centre, Tomide had played several movie jail scenes in his head.

He was photographed and fingerprinted and told he could make one phone call. When he saw the time, he decided against calling James. His friend would not appreciate a middle of the night call. The officer agreed that he could make his call later in the morning.

The closet-sized cell had a raised bench, a crusty looking toilet, a water fountain and a hand wash basin. Tomide was relieved that he didn't end up in a general population cell. He wasn't one to back down from a fight, but he had a low threshold for pain.

His heart skipped when the cell gate clanged shut behind him. He fought back his tears by taking several deep breaths. This wasn't the place to show weakness.

After he'd used the toilet in the full view of the man pacing the cell across the hallway, Tomide sat on the raised bench.

Back against the wall, knees pulled up, he placed the airplane sized pillow behind his head and covered himself with the thin blanket. Daylight couldn't come fast enough.

An hour later, the clinking sound of the cell gate woke him up. Disoriented, Tomide fell off the bench.

"Breakfast," the officer said as he walked through the open gate and held out a cellophane-wrapped sandwich.

Tomide didn't want any food, but he figured it was best to accept it. "Thank you. Please, what time is it?"

The officer's response was curt. "5:00 a.m."

It felt like he had been there for a long time. "Please, when do I get to see the judge?"

"Someone will come and get you."

Several hours passed before he was moved from the cell. The room he landed in had a door leading to the side of a courtroom.

The judge told Tomide his trial would hold in three months' time. The bail conditions were clear. He'd lost the right to enter his house without a police escort or to go anywhere near Titilope and T.J. The judge didn't care that the house was in his name.

Since he didn't have the money to post his bail, he called James.

"Hello?" James sounded like he hadn't gotten much sleep either.

"Hey, it's Tomide. I'm at the detention centre. I need your help."

"I've been waiting to hear from you. What happened between you and Titilope?"

He was sure they'd put a bug on the phone. "We'll talk when you get here. Please, I need some bail money. I can't use my credit card."

"How much?"

"$20,000. Cash." Even though he was a first-time offender, because of Titilope's injuries, the judge had asked for a steep fine. He also had to surrender both his American and Nigerian passports.

James swore. "Where am I meant to find that kind of money?"

He didn't have it either. He'd have to take cash advances from several credit cards to settle the debt. "Please, I'll pay you back before the end of the week."

James sighed. "I may have to talk to my bank about a short-term loan. I'll show up as soon as I get the money."

It was almost 3:00 p.m. before he saw James' face. "Sorry, some things came up at work," James said.

He was grateful James had come through for him. "Bro, I owe you big time."

James waited outside while he completed the necessary paperwork. Twelve hours after his ordeal began, Tomide was a somewhat free man.

Inside the car, James turned to him. "I saw Titilope's face. Were you still angry with her for not making us pepper soup?"

He'd not intended to let things go as far as they did. The goading gleam in Titilope's eyes had pushed him over the edge.

"No. When I got home, Titilope started a fight. She was embarrassed about your intervention. I tried to get away. She followed. She told me she would call the police and have me thrown out of the house. It got to a point I felt this rage come over me and I snapped." Tomide shook his head. "I just snapped."

James sighed. "You should have walked out of the house. Where will you stay?"

"A cheap motel until I sort out my finances."

"T.J.'s staying with us. Titilope was taken to the hospital."

He lowered his eyes. "I can't go near either of them. How's T.J. doing?"

"Bunmi took the day off. He refused to leave her side."

He pictured T.J.'s angry little face as he got between him and Titilope. T.J. had shouted at him to leave his mother alone. "Please tell Bunmi I said thank you."

James shook his head. "It's best I don't mention your name around her."

"I understand."

James tapped his fingers on the steering wheel. "I need the money back by the end of the week. I made the withdrawal from our line of credit. I didn't tell Bunmi."

She would have told her husband no deal. "You have my word."

James ran his hands over his face before he turned on the car engine. "I have to get back to work."

After he'd picked up some fast food, James dropped him off at a nearby motel. The only attraction was the $35 per night rate advertised on the message board sign.

Tomide walked around the room. There was a stale tobacco smell, some suspicious-looking stains on the white bed sheet, but there was hot water and a fresh bar of soap.

After a long shower, he washed his clothes and hung them on the shower curtain rod. He wrapped a towel around his waist, sat on the bed and ate some of his soggy fries.

Back in Nigeria, one of his uncles had always said that a fool at forty was a fool forever. At forty-five, his foolishness at picking women prone to marital strife had landed him on the wrong side of town.

Tomide dumped the rest of the food in the trash can, sprawled on the bed and turned on the television. He needed something to remind him that he wasn't the only one dealing with troubles. The news didn't disappoint. He fell asleep in the middle of an apartment building fire report.

CHAPTER FOURTEEN

Titilope fought tears as she leaned against the vehicle. The overnight observation visit had turned into an excruciating eight-day stay. She had a concussion, a lacerated liver, five fractured ribs and a broken jaw. Her two front teeth were also gone.

A sharp pain shot through her side as she tried to stand on her own. She should have taken the painkillers when her nurse had offered them. Instead, she'd told herself she needed the pain to stay sharp. *You see yourself now?* The mocking voice in her head asked.

Titilope mumbled a response under her breath. "I know I was stupid. Now, zip it."

"Were you talking to me?" Bunmi asked as she slammed the car door shut and swung the strap of Titilope's duffle bag over her left shoulder.

"No. Just thinking aloud."

Bunmi gave a concerned look as she wavered on her feet. "Are you sure you don't need me to hold your hand?"

"I can go up the steps by myself."

Somehow, she made it up the porch steps. Tears flooded her eyes when she walked into a fresh smelling home. When she had mentioned her fear of coming back to blood splattered walls, Bunmi offered to clean. She turned to her friend. "Thank you."

"You're welcome. *Oya*, straight to the couch. You don't need to cook. I made some Jollof rice, chicken stew, and *egusi* soup. The bowls are in your fridge. Since I know how you are, this time I packed them in disposable pans."

Titilope smiled as she settled against propped up couch pillows. Bunmi often joked about how the Tupperware containers sent over to her house never made it back. "You should have raided my drawers when you came over to clean."

Bunmi sat beside her. "It's not too late to get my property. I'll be back tomorrow."

She'd always known Bunmi was a faithful friend. The past week proved the depth of her generosity. "*Ore*, how do I thank you?"

Tears filled Bunmi's eyes. "I introduced you to Tomide."

She reached for her friend's hand. Bunmi brought James and Tomide to her thirtieth birthday party. Newly divorced, Tomide had made it clear he was looking for a wife. After a nasty break-up with her college boyfriend, Titilope was ready to move on.

Dating Tomide was fun. And as far as her parents were concerned, their shared tribal and national identity made Tomide both Mr. Right and Mr. Right-On-Time.

"Please, don't blame yourself. I said yes to the marriage proposal."

"Thank God, you're free now," Bunmi said.

Titilope looked away. Tomide wouldn't walk away without a fight.

Bunmi hung around for another hour. After she had left, Titilope called Amy. The worker had promised that T.J. would come home when she did. She left a message on Amy's voicemail.

Too tired to walk upstairs, Titilope curled up on the long couch. The ringing cell phone woke her. "Hello?"

"Please, may I speak with Titilope Ojo?"

The stranger's voice filled her with disappointment. "Speaking."

"My name's Becky. I'm calling from Victim Services."

One of the police officers had told her she would receive a call from the office. Becky ran through the list of services available to her. Counselling, criminal injuries compensation for lost income, referrals to social service agencies; the information made Titilope's head spin.

"I understand you have a young child?" Becky said.

"Yes."

"Well, my recommendation is that you stop by the courthouse and file a protective order application."

She sat up, grabbing her left side as if she could decrease the pain. "Is Tomide out?"

"Yes. He made bail the day after the incident."

The tight feeling in Titilope's chest led to a bout of coughing. She thought he'd still be in police custody. "Can he take my son?"

"A protective order will give you temporary custody of your child. He wouldn't be able to attend your home, workplace or contact you in any way. If he does, he'll be arrested and taken back to jail."

"Please, may I have your contact information? I'll come to the courthouse first thing in the morning."

"Sure."

Titilope found a pen and notebook in her purse and scribbled down the information.

"If Mr. Ojo comes to the house, please call 911."

"Thank you."

The ball of fear in her chest grew after she ended the phone call. Would a piece of paper keep Tomide away from her? She was sure he kept spare house keys at the office. What if he came by while she was asleep?

She'd contacted a locksmith through an online listing when Amy called her back. "Is it okay for me to get T.J. now?"

"We're not restricting your access. However, there are some things I need to discuss with you."

Titilope squirmed in her seat. She'd hoped CPS would leave them alone since Tomide was out of the house. "What things?"

"We'll discuss them when we meet."

"Fine."

"I'm sure you're not in the best shape to drive. How about I pick you up, and we can talk on our way to the day care?"

"Thank you. I'll be waiting for you."

During the drive, Amy told her the agency had submitted a court application for a supervision order.

At the word 'court', a wave of nausea ran through her. "You've changed your mind about letting T.J. come home?"

Amy shook her head. "No. The order would allow us to monitor T.J.'s safety and well-being."

"He's safe with me."

"Given the seriousness of what happened, we think this plan is in T.J.'s best interest. I know there are all a lot of misconceptions about CPS workers. I truly want to support your family through all this. How can I help?"

By disappearing. Titilope stared at her hands. "Right now, I need to hold my son and take him home."

"We'll continue this discussion at a different time."

T.J.'s left thumb was in his mouth, Mr. Bear clutched in his right hand when they arrived at the day care. Titilope exchanged a look with Ms. Paula. T.J. had stopped sucking his finger when he was two. "Hey, T.J.," Titilope said.

His face lit up as he turned away from the window "Mum!"

She fell to her knees and braced herself for the impact as he ran towards her.

"Are we going home?" T.J. asked when he saw Amy standing by the doorway.

Tears ran down Titilope's face. "Yes, sweetie. We're going home."

CHAPTER FIFTEEN

On the morning of the protection order hearing, Titilope kept her eyes on the mounted emblem above the judge's bench. From where he sat, Tomide's eyes bore into her.

After they both took the stand and gave their testimonies, the judge gave his ruling. Titilope listened with bated breath as the judge awarded her custody of T.J. and ordered Tomide to pay child support. Her body shook from an overwhelming feeling of victory.

When she snuck a glance at Tomide's face, he looked as if he was going to cry. The judge ordered supervised access visits with T.J. until Tomide had completed a 52-week anger management class.

She stared ahead when the judge cleared his throat. "Mr. Ojo."

Tomide stood. "Yes, Your Honour."

"Do you understand the terms and conditions of this order?"

"Yes, Your Honour."

He gave Tomide a stern look. "The order is for one year. It will remain in effect until the date which would be in the document provided to you. Violating an order is a criminal offense. If you do, it will lead to an arrest."

The judge turned in her direction. "Mrs. Ojo?"

Titilope jumped to her feet. "Yes, Your Honour."

"It is your responsibility to notify the police if Mr. Ojo violates any part of the order by contacting you, re-abusing you or entering your residence or workplace."

He gave her a warning look. "I'm aware couples often reconcile after these domestic incidents. While the court remains neutral on such decisions, we don't endorse violations. The dismissal or modification of the protective order requires a request in writing and a subsequent ruling by a judge. Am I clear?"

She gripped the edge of the table. "Yes, Your Honour."

***

Titilope's heart pounded as she opened her eyes and looked around the bedroom. The eerie feeling that there was someone else in the room woke her. She was alone.

She walked across the hallway and found T.J. fast asleep. She stooped to pick up his blanket from the floor and covered him.

Even though she'd checked the windows and doors at least a dozen times before they went upstairs, Titilope walked around the house and made sure her newly installed alarm system was working.

She decided to make herself a cup of chamomile tea. Perhaps it'd help her sleep. After she had brewed the tea, she sat at the kitchen table and took a sip.

"Mum?"

The fear in T.J.'s voice made her hurry to the bottom of the stairs. "Sweetie, I'm here."

Mr. Bear came down with him. There were tears on his face. "I went to your room, and I didn't see you."

She had moved T.J. to his bed after he fell asleep in hers. They curled up on the couch. "What's wrong?" she asked.

He looked sadly at her. "Everything is different."

Titilope stroked his head. "Different can be good."

"I miss Dad."

T.J.'s feelings about his father were mixed. Earlier in the day, T.J. had refused to attend his supervised access visit with Tomide.

"I'm sure he misses you too."

"I didn't want to go see Dad because I think he's mad at me."

"Why would he be mad at you?"

T.J. gave her his old man frown. "Because I called the number and the police officer put those things on Dad's hands when they came."

Titilope wished the police officers had not handcuffed Tomide in front of T.J. He couldn't stop talking about it.

She felt his body shake. "Sweetie, look at me." T.J. lifted a wet face. "What happened was not your fault. You did the right thing by calling for help."

He didn't look convinced. "Pete said I'm now the man of the house."

Pete was one of his day care buddies. "Are you going to get a big boy job and pay half of the bills? If you are, the cable bill is due."

T.J. rolled his eyes. "Little kids can't get jobs."

"That's right. Little kids are not supposed to take care of the adults. It's my job to take care of you."

T.J.'s voice shook. "Since you said Dad's not mad at me, can I go see him on Saturday?"

Although she didn't want Tomide anywhere near him, she'd accepted her son's need to see his father. "Yes."

T.J. buried his face in her nightshirt.

***

The next day, James came for the rest of Tomide's things. At his request, they sat at the kitchen table to talk.

"Titilope, I must let you know I'm disappointed by your behaviour."

It was the last thing she'd expected him to say. "Excuse me?"

James shook his head. "This isn't how we deal with these issues. If you were reluctant to tell me what was going on, you should have reported Tomide to his mother."

"The woman he has no respect for?"

"You could have told our community elders. They would have provided some immediate intervention. A felony conviction will cost Tomide his security clearance. You know he can't do his job without one. How will he take care of his sons? Please, Titilope. Drop the criminal charges. I've spoken to him. He's remorseful."

She fought the urge to walk James out. "I didn't lay the charges. The police did."

"If you'd refused to testify against him, the case would have gone away. Think about the impact on T.J."

"I think about it every day. I know how much Tomide's abusive behaviour scarred my child."

"All marriages go through trying periods."

She held up a hand. "You saw what Tomide did to me."

"He said he snapped."

Titilope snickered. "Rubber bands and twigs snap. Tomide knew what he was doing."

"What Tomide did was wrong. But, all human beings are flawed. One must learn to forgive and move on."

"I've heard what you said."

As her mother often told her, there was a marked difference between, 'I've heard what you said' and 'I'm willing to comply with your request.'

From the look on his face, James could tell her response didn't signify compliance. "Titilope, your hands are not clean," he said.

"What do you mean by that?"

"Tomide showed me the scars on his arms. He told me about how you mutilate yourself and hurt him when he's trying to help. This time you pushed him too far."

She held up her hands. "Yes, those scars came from my nails. I keep them long to defend myself."

James gasped. "Tomide told me the truth?"

"Half-truth. That's how your best friend operates. He's an expert at mixing a little truth with a lot of lies. Tell me, if you were in my shoes, what would you have done? Would you have asked him to explain why your life has less value than his?"

Titilope gave herself a light smack on the forehead. "Silly me. I should know how hard it is to carry a conversation when someone has their hands wrapped around your neck."

James opened his mouth. After what looked like a futile search for words, he closed it.

Tired of the conversation, Titilope stood up and pushed back her chair. "Thank you for everything. Please, tell Bunmi I said hello."

***

Right in the middle of T.J.'s favourite television show, they were startled by the loud chime of the doorbell. They weren't expecting anyone.

Titilope held him close as they shuffled their way to the front door. She looked out through the peephole and saw a friendly face.

"It's Aunty Holly," she said to T.J. before she opened the door.

The blood drained from Holly's face. "What happened? Were you in an accident?"

"No. Please come in. I guess you're here to pick up Jordan's things?"

Holly stepped inside. "Yes. Tommy called and said he no longer lives here. I thought you'd finally—"

Her son didn't need to hear any of the adult stuff. "We'll talk about that later. T.J., you haven't said hello to Aunty Holly."

Holly gave Titilope an apologetic look. "Hi, Buddy."

T.J. stepped forward for a hug. "Hi, Aunty."

"I've missed your face," Holly said.

"Sweetie, please go and watch your program while Aunty Holly and I get your brother's things."

T.J. skipped away.

They were in Jordan's bedroom when she gave Holly a quick update.

Holly took a deep breath. "Tommy is such an ass. I'm glad you're still here. Do you guys need anything? I can make a quick run to the store."

"We have enough food for now. Jordan is welcome here. You don't need to pack up his things."

Holly gave her grateful smile. "Call when you have the energy for both boys. You know T.J.'s also welcome at our place."

"I know. When things calm down, we'll plan a sleepover."

At the door, Holly gave her another hug. "This changes nothing between us. We're family, right?"

Titilope smiled. "Yes, we are."

CHAPTER SIXTEEN

Tomide stood as he surveyed his new home. The studio apartment wasn't even as big as his basement man cave. He'd been lucky to stumble upon the "House Sitter Wanted" ad on his work bulletin board. The guy was spending a year in China and didn't want his apartment to stay empty. Apart from the regular upkeep, all he had to do was pay the utility bills.

The pressure cooker's whistle drew him to the stove. He turned it off, placed the pot in the kitchen sink and turned on the tap. After he had run the pot under a jet of cold water, he opened the lid, stirred the pottage and tasted it for salt. It was perfect. Tomide puffed out his chest. Due to his regular cooking, his one-pot meal skills had improved. Fewer things to wash, more leftovers to eat.

He dished his food, arranged everything on a tray and sat in front of the television to watch basketball. He couldn't focus. Without his boys, game nights didn't feel the same.

While he debated on what else to do, the doorbell rang. He set his tray down and walked over the door. "Who is it?"

"It's James."

When he opened the door, his friend walked in with two large suitcases.

"My *numero uno padi*. I was just thinking about you."

James dropped the suitcases by his feet. "You know I'm a genuine son of my father."

"DNA test not required." He gave his friend a grateful smile. "Thanks for bringing my stuff. I couldn't get to you yesterday."

James sat while Tomide moved the suitcases near his bed. "I just cooked some wicked yam and plantain pottage, should I make you a plate?"

"No, thanks. I'm sure Bunmi has made dinner."

He smacked his lips. "Hmm, you're missing out."

"Next time."

James' serious expression made him uneasy. "Did something happen to one of my boys?"

"Tomide, what led to the scars on your hands?"

Mrs. Canary had done some more singing. Tomide weighed his options. The way he saw it, he only had two. One, continue with his effective smear campaign. Two, admit to his actions and throw himself at James' mercy. He was getting tired of lying.

"I caused them. Titilope was only defending herself."

James' hands went to the top of his head. "She doesn't mutilate herself?"

"No."

James flinched. "Tomide, why?"

For the first time, Tomide gave much thought to his behaviour. When he felt challenged, he lashed out to re-establish his authority.

Tomide's thoughts drifted to his father. There could be some genetic mutation. "Perhaps it's a case of like father, like son," he said.

James looked at him as if he was dirt. "First, you told me, I can't hurt a woman because of what my father did to my mother. Now, you say my father's genes are responsible. Man, own your stupidity."

A part of him wished he hadn't opened the door. "I know I need help. And I'm working on it."

"You lied to me," James said as if until that moment, he had not entertained the thought. "I defended you. I even hid things from my wife. I should have 'senior *mumu*' branded on my forehead."

The words brought genuine remorse. James was like the brother he never had. "I'm sorry."

James' gaze grew cold. "Save your apologies for your wife and son. I'm going home."

***

Sometime after midnight, Tomide called Nigeria. With the five-hour time difference, his mother, an early riser, would be awake. He'd decided to report himself with the hope that she would get Titilope's mother to plead his case.

His mother's voice was thick with sleep when she picked the call. "Who is this?"

"*Ekaaro*, Ma."

"Tomide, is that you?" she asked.

He knew his calls home were irregular, but how could she not recognise her son's voice? "Yes, Ma."

Her voice became alarmed. "What happened? How are your wife and sons?"

Tomide shifted his body on the bed as T.J.'s face came to his mind. "They're all fine."

His mother sighed her relief. "Then why are you not asleep?" she asked.

"I had to discuss an important matter with you," he said.

Her voice grew suspicious. "What is it?"

"Last week, I made a huge mistake. The police arrested me."

"Ha! Police? What did you do?"

"Titilope and I had a little fight. She ended up in the hospital."

"*E gba mi*. Tomide, what kind of little fight lands your wife at the hospital?"

He exhaled with a deep sigh. "I was angry. I wasn't thinking."

"Tomide, I've always told you that anger destroys things," his mother said in a chiding tone.

The automatic response came out. "I'm sorry, Ma."

"You have not done well at all. Is Titilope awake? Give her the phone."

"Titilope is not with me. The police said I had to leave the house."

"You had to leave the house?"

Her shock was evident. "Yes, Ma."

"Since you made this mistake, it is right for you to leave. When things get to this stage, it is best for a couple to be apart for a while. Distance will cool things down."

He had come to the uncomfortable conclusion that they needed something other than distance.

"You have not done well at all. Let this be the first and only incident. Have you heard?"

He could not tell her about the other times. "I'm sorry, Ma."

"Sorry for yourself," she snapped. "Tomide, when you left Mama Jordan, you told us it was because she didn't like us, your family. Now, what has Titilope done that you want to kill her? This behaviour you took from your father will chase your wife away."

Tomide clenched his jaw. "I'm trying to make things better. Your husband did nothing, and you stayed with him."

His mother sighed. "I will go and see your mother-in-law today. We will figure this out."

"Thank you, Ma."

"Don't thank me yet. Pray that your in-laws don't decide to blow your foolish nose like a trumpet. *Omo a ko ni si'ta bi omo ojo mejo.*"

The rebuke stung. Before Tomide could respond, his mother disconnected the call.

Tomide flung the cell phone across the room. It bounced off the wall and broke into pieces.

CHAPTER SEVENTEEN

Mrs. Tamuno gave Titilope a welcoming smile as she stepped into their favourite African store. "Mrs. Ojo, long time, no see."

She'd kept away because Tomide borrowed his Nollywood movies from the store. "Yes. Blame it on this busy American life."

Mrs. Tamuno nodded. "God help us as we chase this hide-and-seek dollar. How is my little friend?"

T.J. enjoyed the free snacks Mrs. Tamuno gave him. "He's doing fine. I hope you have his plantain chips in stock."

"They came in yesterday."

"Perfect timing." Titilope headed for the snack aisle.

Mrs. Tamuno had bagged her purchases when two women walked into the store. Titilope's heart sank. The first, Efe, was married to Tomide's friend. She had met the other woman at one of the many Nigerian summer parties. She couldn't remember her name.

Efe's eyes widened when she saw her. "Titilope. You're still in this city?"

At best, she and Efe tolerated each other. "Someone told you I moved?"

Efe shook her head. "No one tells me anything."

She gave Efe a tight-lipped smile, thanked Mrs. Tamuno and picked up her shopping bags. "I have to go. Take care."

Efe moved aside as she walked out of the store.

Out in the parking lot, Titilope realised she'd dropped her keys near the stack of plantain chips. The thought of another meeting with Efe made her sigh. She headed back.

Engrossed in her conversation, Efe didn't look her way when she walked into the store.

Mrs. Tamuno did. The store owner stayed silent when their eyes met.

"What happened between them?" The other woman asked Efe.

"You can't repeat this to anyone," Efe said as if they were alone.

"Never."

"My husband told me Tomide woke up and found Titilope standing over him with a kitchen knife."

The woman placed both hands on her chest. "What was she going to do with the knife?"

"What do you think? Peel yam? If not for Tomide's agility, we'd have been singing 'Till We Meet at Jesus' feet' at his celebration of life."

"Tomide's such a good man too."

"He is. He said questioning Titilope's promiscuous behaviour led to the incident."

Titilope clenched her jaw. Tomide was relentless in his smear campaign.

"*Eh hen?* But Titilope doesn't strike me as that type."

Efe snorted. "Don't let her standoffish look fool you. Women like her are perfect mistress material. The heat they radiate from their core will melt any man's resolve."

The other woman gave Efe a sceptical look. "Any man?"

"If you don't believe me, send your husband over to help Titilope change her out-of-reach lightbulbs. He will appreciate your generous gesture."

Titilope snickered. Sometimes, silence made fools like Efe think they'd been given wings to fly. To get the women's attention, she cleared her throat.

Efe took a backward step after her head swung in Titilope's direction. "You came back?"

She gave Efe a tight-lipped smile. "Thanks for the referral. I do have a burnt lightbulb. Last week, it was so kind of your husband to help with my plumbing needs. Without proper attention, some places get clogged."

Efe's purse dropped from her hand. "What did you say?"

Titilope smirked. "I was speaking English."

Efe hurled insults at her.

"Madam Efe, please, this is a place of business," Mrs. Tamuno said in a firm voice.

"You should be careful about the kind of people you sell things to," Efe said.

"I treat all my customers with respect. How would you like to pay for your purchases?" Mrs. Tamuno asked.

Efe threw up her hands. "Forget it. Keep your *ashawo* customer. You're not the only African store around here."

Titilope's heart pounded as Efe tugged on her friend's arm and they walked out. She took one look at the food items Efe had left behind, Mrs. Tamuno's face, and she burst into tears. "I'm sorry."

Mrs. Tamuno walked over to the storefront window, flipped the open sign, locked the door and brought two tall stools from behind the counter. "You did nothing wrong. Please, sit down."

Too numb to speak, Titilope sat with her head bowed.

"I know what happened with your husband," Mrs. Tamuno said.

Her head flew up. "You do?"

Mrs. Tamuno gave her a guilty look. "One of us works at the hospital. She was there when the ambulance brought you in."

Titilope wasn't surprised by the breach of privacy. In their community, confidentiality was still a foreign concept. "I can't understand why women like Efe are so vicious."

"It's a mix of bitterness and jealousy. You have what some other women want. Freedom." Mrs. Tamuno stood. "Let me get you something."

Titilope watched as Mrs. Tamuno pulled a business card from her wallet. She came back and handed it over. "I volunteer at a Women's Centre here in Rockville. I think you'll find their services useful."

Titilope took the card. "Thank you."

"If there's anything else I can do to help, please, don't hesitate to contact me."

Titilope's eyes filled with fresh tears. "I won't forget your offer."

"Good." Mrs. Tamuno gave her a soft smile. "Now, what brought you back?"

***

Titilope yawned as she closed the bathroom door. She had to be up in three hours. She was back under her warm blanket when the telephone rang. She shot the device a look of annoyance. Only one person called her in the middle of the night. The time difference meant nothing to her mother. She called whenever she wanted.

Her voice was gruff with annoyance when she answered the call. "Hello?"

"*Omo mi*, how are you?"

It was Tomide's mother. "*Ekaaro*, Ma."

"Tomide just told me what he did to you," she said.

Surprised by the words, Titilope sat up. Tomide told someone the truth?

"My daughter, believe me, I'm on my knees. Please, forgive me. It's my fault. I failed to raise a good man."

"Mummy, what Tomide did wasn't your fault. Yes, our parents raise us but we also have to raise ourselves."

Her mother-in-law gave a loud sigh. "Titilope."

"Ma."

"Child, your days will be long."

"*Amin*, Ma."

"Listen, I didn't call to tell you what to do. Yes, Tomide's my only son, but you and T.J. belong to me too. I don't believe in sacrificing one child for the benefit of the other. Have you told your parents about the incident?"

Now that Tomide's mother knew, she'd have to call before the news got to them. "No, Ma."

"Don't worry. I'll call your mother."

"Thank you, Ma."

About fifteen minutes later, the phone rang. Titilope picked it up. "Hello?"

"Titilope?"

She wondered what her mother would say if she said, "No, wrong number." She let out a deep breath. "Yes, Ma."

"Your mother-in-law called me. I heard Tomide went to jail because of you."

"I didn't send him there. He sent himself."

"When Mama Tomide told me, I thought to myself, no woman worth her weight in salt will send the father of her child to jail."

She had known her mother would say forgive and move on.

"Did Mama Tomide tell you he sent me to the hospital? I stayed longer at the hospital than he stayed inside a jail cell."

"She mentioned a hospital visit," Mummy saidin a vague tone.

"I guess you'll be satisfied when he ships my dead body back to you."

Mummy's voice rose. "Dead body *ke*? God forbid. Anyone who wants to kill you would have to kill me first." Her voice became soothing. "Of course, I don't want you to die. Titilope, you're my joy."

For the second time that morning, her eyes filled with tears. "Mummy, you have no idea how hard it has been."

"Please, don't cry. Mama Tomide said your husband is not living at home. Titilope, the tongue, and teeth fight all the time. Have you ever heard that one of them left the mouth due to unresolved anger? Go and tell the police you're ready for Tomide to come back home. He will change his ways."

"Mummy, Tomide's never going to change. How can he, when he thinks he doesn't have a problem?"

"People change all the time. His mother and I will put our heads together and come up with a solution."

There was nothing they could do for her. "Mummy, I have to work in the morning."

"Ha, I just noticed the time. *Oya*, go back to sleep. *Asunji o.*"

Titilope was still awake when her alarm went off. It was going to be a long day.

CHAPTER EIGHTEEN

Tomide sat with his head in his hands. As part of the plea agreement with the district attorney's office, he'd pled guilty to the domestic violence charges. The deal led to zero jail time and a case dismissal after he'd completed two years of probation and 100 hours of community service.

After several meetings with their HR personnel, he'd not lost his job. However, due to internal disciplinary measures, he was moved to a new role. He hated it. If not for the conviction, he would have left. But few employers would hire an employee with a criminal record. He had to wait until his probation was over.

The only thing he had to look forward to was getting back with Titilope. Tomide stood from the couch and grabbed his new cell phone. His mother had told him to call at the end of the week for an update.

"Please, Ma, what did my mother-in-law say?"

"She said her daughter no longer wants the marriage."

When did Titilope become so hard-headed? "Please, talk to her. She might listen to you."

"Tomide, if you want your wife back, the rest is up to you."

"But the judge said I cannot have any contact with her."

"Is that my fault? We raise children with the hope that they'll give us peace in our old age. The good Lord bears witness to how much I laboured over you. I'm going to sleep."

In the past, he wouldn't have hesitated to contact James for advice. But their relationship was yet to recover from the lies he'd told. Conversations between them were short as James couldn't wait to get off the phone. Desperate, he dialled James' home number.

Bunmi picked the call. "Hello?"

For a moment, he was speechless. He'd not spoken to Bunmi since the incident. "*Em*, hi. It's Tomide."

"*Eh-hen*?"

"Is James home?"

He heard her sharp intake of air. "Yes. Next time, call his cell phone."

"What do you want?" James asked when he took the call.

The hostile tone made Tomide's shoulders slump. "Are things this bad between us?'

"I've accepted your apology. I still think it's best we keep our distance."

"I'll get to the point. I need a chance to talk to Titilope. I want to apologize. I can't meet with her unless she writes a letter to my probation officer saying she wants the 'no contact' condition lifted. I'm hoping Bunmi will plead my case."

"I don't want my wife dragged into that mess. She's done enough for you. If you want to speak to Titilope, you'll have to find someone else. I do think you're wasting your time."

His fingers clenched around the phone. "Is Titilope dating someone? We're still married."

"Whether she is or not, is none of my business," James said.

The response made him feel uneasy. "Brother, please."

"I need to go."

"Thank you."

Tomide ended the call. He spent the next hour pacing the room and thinking of a new action plan.

***

There was a strange car parked in Holly's driveway with a Delaware license plate. As far as Tomide remembered, Holly didn't have family living in that state.

Male laughter drifted out through the open windows as he walked up to the house. Who was visiting?

He pressed the doorbell and Holly answered it. "I see you have company."

She didn't invite him in. "Yes."

"Family?"

Holly stepped outside and closed the door behind her. "No. Jordan will be out soon."

He cleared his throat. "If this person is spending time with my son, I think it's important I meet him."

Holly snorted. "When did you tell me about Titilope?"

He hadn't said anything to Holly until about a month to his second wedding. And it was because Jordan needed to buy a suit. "This man is your boyfriend?"

Holly shrugged. "I don't owe you an explanation."

Tomide took a deep breath as he visualised himself on a walk down a country road. The therapist who ran his anger management class had stressed the importance of walking away from emotions which encourage anger outbursts. He knew he was jealous and fearful of the time this man spent with Jordan. He didn't want to lose any part of Jordan's love.

He took a step back. "You're right."

Holly narrowed her eyes. "You're not going to beat your chest and barge in to check out this man?"

A part of him wanted to. "I'll meet him when you think the time's right."

Holly looked up at the sky. "I guess we're going to get a blue moon tonight."

Tomide forced a smile. "Please tell Jordan I'll wait for him in the car. See you on Sunday."

***

Jordan's face lit up when he walked into the apartment and saw the camping tent Tomide had set up in the middle of the living room. "You remembered."

During his last visit, Jordan said he couldn't wait for summer so he could go camping with his scout group. "You like it?"

"Yeah! Are we going to roast some marshmallows?"

He'd found a new recipe online. "In the oven."

Jordan gave him a tight hug. "Thanks, Dad."

After he had made them some chocolate-covered marshmallows and hot dogs, they sat inside the tent. "I like this," Jordan said.

Tomide nodded his agreement.

"I wish T.J. was here," Jordan said in a wistful tone.

Tomide swallowed the lump Jordan's words had brought to his throat. The weekly one-hour supervised visits with T.J. were not enough.

He ruffled Jordan's hair. "Guess what? You can take the tent home. When T.J. comes over, you guys can camp inside."

Jordan's face brightened up. "I guess. But Mum doesn't like us making a mess."

"She'll say yes if you clean up your mess on time."

Jordan cocked his head to the side. "Dad, can we have another man talk?"

Tomide felt his mouth go dry. He'd promised Jordan he'd always tell the truth during their man talks. The truth as he knew it. "Yes."

"T.J. said he couldn't come here because you had hurt Aunty Titilope."

"That's true."

Jordan looked puzzled. "Why did you hurt her?"

He could finally admit why. "Because I've always wanted my way. And I don't like hearing no."

"Oh. Do you still always want your way?"

Tomide sighed. One of the questions his counsellor had asked him was, what does a life worth living look like to you. His current state was far from that of an ideal husband or father. "Sometimes. I'm working hard on it. You can tell T.J. this. I'm never going to hurt his mum again."

Jordan looked solemn. "Promise?"

"I do."

Jordan smiled. "Can we watch a movie now?"

He wished other issues in his life were that easy to resolve. "Yes, we can."

CHAPTER NINETEEN

Titilope left work early and headed to Academy Way Women's Centre for the introductory meeting with a counsellor. Heated conversations with her mother had caused several sleepless nights. Drained, she'd dug out the business card Mrs. Tamuno gave her and called for help. She also unplugged her home phone at night.

Titilope parked in the secure lot and walked up to the two-story brick building. The discrete metal sign posted beside the front door confirmed she was at the right place.

As directed, Titilope pressed the entry buzzer, stepped back and stared into the security camera. She heard a woman's voice. "Name please."

"Titilope Ojo. I'm here to meet with Sunbeam."

"Please come in."

The steel door clicked open. Titilope pulled the door handle and walked into what looked like a doctor's waiting room. The woman standing there greeted her with a warm smile. "Hey, you made it. I'm Sunbeam. Come on in."

Titilope tried to mask her surprise. The soft, girly voice she'd heard on the phone didn't match this tattoo-covered woman whose silver streaked, blonde dreadlocks hung down to her waist. She shook the offered hand. "I'm sorry for being late. I missed my way."

"That's alright. The most important thing is that you're here."

They walked up to another set of double steel doors, and Sunbeam unlocked it with an entry card. It was not this difficult for Titilope to get into her bank building.

As if Sunbeam had read her mind, she said, "Safety's our number one priority. We've had some pretty disgruntled people show up at our door. They don't do well with the word 'no'."

"I can imagine," Titilope said with a sigh.

"Before we sit for a chat, I'll give you a grand tour of our premises."

Sunbeam explained their services as she took Titilope through the shelter area which housed ten women and their children. They walked down a short flight of stairs to a basement auditorium.

Titilope looked around. A white flip board with the red words 'No Judgement Zone' stood next to a circle of beige plastic chairs.

"This is where we hold our groups. I'm hoping you will join us."

The thought of sharing her story in front of others made Titilope feel uncomfortable. "I don't think I want to be part of a group. Too many people will know my business."

Sunbeam gave her an understanding look. "Before we start each group session, we agree that everything shared is confidential. Some of our clients live with their abusers and we cannot mess around with safety."

"Are there other options?"

"Oh, yes. We also offer individual sessions. In this place, we honour your wishes. No pressure."

They made their way back upstairs and walked down a new hallway. Sunbeam stopped by a door. It had a poster of a giant, red apple with spiky, green hair.

"Meet Sir Mackintosh," Sunbeam had a twinkle in her eyes as she turned the door handle. "He guards our Kids Club room. These young ones have seen too much, heard too much. Visits here offer them a much-needed outlet."

Titilope looked around the room. A large bowl of apples sat on the oval coffee table. "Someone loves apples," she said.

Sunbeam grinned. "That someone is me. A long time ago, a wise woman, aka my grandma, once told me when you're walking through an orchard and an apple falls on your head, you can either whine about it or pick it up and smile at the free food."

Titilope pondered on the words. "Shifting perspectives."

Sunbeam nodded. "Grandma grew up during the depression. She wasn't going to throw away an apple."

"I also don't believe in waste."

"On the phone, you had mentioned that you have a little boy. He's welcome to join us anytime."

T.J. still had rough days. "Thank you."

Sunbeam pulled out a chair. "We might as well sit here," she said.

Titilope took a deep breath as she sat across from Sunbeam. She wasn't sure where to start.

"Can I get you anything? Water, coffee, tea?" Sunbeam asked.

"No, thank you."

Sunbeam gave her a bright smile. "I have to say your name has a lovely, musical ring to it."

She crossed her legs. "Thank you."

"What does it mean?" Sunbeam asked.

A straight Yoruba to English translation was difficult. "A close meaning is 'forever thanks'."

"That's a unique name."

"Your name is also unique," Titilope said.

Sunbeam grinned. "I was born in the 1960s. My hippie parents, bless their flower power hearts, thought it was cute. At almost 6 feet by seventh grade, I toweredover my classmates. One of the kids in my class said they should have named me Sunblock."

Sunbeam's bubbly personality had melted away some of Titilope's anxiety. "It's a good thing you can laugh about it."

"The ability to laugh at myself has helped me deal with a shipload of shit. Pardon my French. Like I told you on the telephone, I don't have fancy letters behind my name. I started having these conversations as my way of giving back for all the good which came to me when I was in an abusive relationship."

Sunbeam's admission surprised her. "My story isn't pretty," she said.

"There's nothing heart-warming about abuse. It's all up to you. We're not working from a script."

Titilope took a deep breath. "All right."

"There's an ice-breaker activity I do with the women at our first group session. Do you want to give it a try?"

She gave a nervous laugh. "Sure."

"I'd like you to tell me what animal you see yourself as and why. I'll go first. When I had to do the exercise, the animal image which came to my mind shocked me."

"What was it?"

"An ant," Sunbeam said.

The image didn't match the formidable woman in front of her. "Oh."

"Believe me, I've been six-five and weighed over two hundred pounds since I was sixteen." Sunbeam tapped the side of her head. "Right here though, I saw myself an ant. Ordinary, inconsequential, disposable. My boyfriend's fist was the shoe sole poised over me."

An image came to Titilope's mind. A camel? She'd never even seen one. When she thought about it, the image made sense.

"Well, I see myself as a camel. Right now, it feels like I'm journeying through the desert with no oasis in sight. It's an endless sea of sand."

Sunbeam nodded. "Deserts are harsh places. Still, camels have the strength and resilience for their long journey."

Titilope gave a shy smile. "The funny thing is I've always felt that a camel is an ugly animal."

"It depends on who's looking at it. Its appearance is a beautiful sight to those waiting on the precious cargo it carries. Trust me, if I were a desert dweller waiting on my shipment of olive oil to fry some date cakes, a camel would have a lot of value."

Sunbeam's words made sense. "My husband told me I had little value."

"To maintain control, he knew he had to break your spirit," Sunbeam said. "It is easy to abuse someone when we disregard their humanity."

Tomide's words had her encased in a steel trap. "The things he said played in an endless loop inside my head. I believed them."

"Like I tell the women who attend our group, while our trauma experiences are unique, the emotions we feel are often the same. We've all grappled with feelings of confusion, worthlessness, and powerlessness."

In her head, Titilope checked all three boxes.

"I know you're no longer in contact with him but time might come when you would have to maintain some contact because of your child," Sunbeam said. "You should prepare for that."

Titilope squirmed in her seat. "I don't know how."

Sunbeam pulled out a pamphlet from her pocket and handed it over. "This talks about safety planning. It's best to go over your plan before you need it. If you're comfortable sharing or have any questions, we can go over it together."

Titilope scanned through the pamphlet. It stated that for some women, dialling 911 from their home places them at even greater risk. "If they can't call the police, what are they meant to do?"

"They can decide on whom to call and what code words to say so these safe people can call."

Whenever Titilope thought of what might have happened to her if T.J. hadn't called 911, she was thankful for his day care teacher.

She glanced at the clock in the room. Time had flown quickly. "I'm sorry to cut this short. I have to pick up my son."

Sunbeam pulled herself up and held out her hand after Titilope stood. "I'm glad you came. You have my number. Please, call if you need any help. I also go on coffee dates. I'll confess that I'm yet to meet a donut I don't like."

She also liked donuts and this woman who gave her a sense of community. "If it's okay with you, I'll like to make another appointment."

Sunbeam returned her smile. "Those are sweet words to my ears."

CHAPTER TWENTY

While searching through her nightstand drawer for a rebate receipt, Titilope came across the gift certificate Holly gave her for passing the CPA exams. It had no expiration date.

Excited, she called Bunmi and made her commit to a girls' day out. It had been a while since their last one.

On the day of their outing, Bunmi came to her house, and she drove them to the downtown spa. The discrete signage on the all brick building gave it an understated elegance.

"Your senior co-wife has taste," Bunmi said as she unclasped her seat belt.

The co-wife title reminded her of Tomide. "*Abeg*, just call her Holly or Mama Jordan."

Bunmi gave her an apologetic look. "I'm sorry."

"Are you sure the certificate will cover our pedicures?" Bunmi asked as Titilope pushed open the double doors leading into the spa.

"It should cover four people's pedicures."

Bunmi looked around. "Maybe at one of those discount nail bars."

"Relax."

Titilope was disappointed to find out that spa's redemption rules had changed. They couldn't use the gift certificate for a pedicure. The options available to them that day were either a *Vivant* sauna, massage or steam room experience.

She stepped away from the customer desk and had a private conversation with Bunmi. She didn't mind paying the additional fee, but it wasn't what they had planned.

Bunmi was clear. "I'm not sharing any nakedness with strangers. If they have a couple's only room, the steam experience sounds like the best choice."

It turned out that they did have a private room. Titilope and Bunmi showered, wore white monogrammed bathrobes and drank cups of juice before they headed to the steam room. They walked into the bamboo panelled space and sat on opposite benches.

Titilope relaxed as the steamy mist wrapped her in an embrace. "This feels good."

Bunmi rested her back against the wall. "It does. This is why I try not to expose myself to the rich people life. I don't need any unnecessary longing."

"There's nothing wrong with occasional treats," Titilope said.

"Thanks for bringing me."

"It's my little way of saying thanks for standing by me."

"Sometimes I feel as if I'm not doing enough," Bunmi said.

"Trust me, you are."

"Then why didn't you tell me you had the 'no contact' condition removed?"

During his last parent-teacher meeting, T.J. cried because they couldn't be in the same room. After a conversation with Tomide's probation officer, she'd gone back to court and had the condition lifted. Tomide's visits with T.J. also became unsupervised.

Titilope sighed. "I didn't think you would approve. And I needed to do it for T.J."

"You should do what is best for your child. I just don't want you to get hurt again. Tomide called James to tell him. He thinks it's a sign that you want him back."

"Perhaps I can ask James to explain things to him."

Bunmi sighed. "Their friendship suffered a major hit. Even though Tomide told James he is not the same man, James insists things cannot go back to the way they were."

Titilope could relate with James' position. "Dishonesty is not an easy thing to deal with," she said.

"Are you still going to counselling?" Bunmi asked.

Bunmi had expressed her surprise when Titilope told her about Sunbeam. It took a while for Bunmi to understand that she needed an objective sounding board. "Yes."

"I'm impressed. A counsellor would have to hypnotise me to get me to talk."

Titilope smiled. "You may surprise yourself."

Her first session with Sunbeam was an awkward one. She had dropped T.J. at Holly's and met with Sunbeam for a late evening appointment. The soft yellow glow of the lamp in the room made it easy to hide her face in the shadows.

Bunmi didn't look convinced. "You sit down and she tells you how to run your life?"

"No. Sunbeam guides the conversation and offers alternatives. On some days, she just listens to me rant. I decide on my next steps."

"Hmm. So, have you decided on what to do?"

The other day T.J. came home and told her that he didn't want to be the child of divorced people. She hadn't asked him where he heard the word. It was a reality of the times for her four-year-old.

Titilope struggled with twofold guilt. By staying with Tomide, she had exposed T.J. to the violence. She also didn't want to grant her son's wish by taking Tomide back. As far as T.J. was concerned Tomide had changed and deserved a second chance.

Titilope closed her eyes as she leaned against the bamboo panels. "Not yet," she said.

CHAPTER TWENTY-ONE

The telephone rang in the middle of dinner. Titilope ignored it. After several minutes, T.J. looked at her. "Mum, do you want me to get the phone?"

"I'll get it." Titilope pushed back her dining chair. She sighed with relief when she heard the recording. It was a telemarketing company.

She'd been worried it was her mother. Although their conversations were in Yoruba, T.J. could tell the calls distressed her.

As she washed the dishes, Titilope decided that they needed a break from Rockville. She'd always wanted to visit Ocean City. T.J. loved water, and it wasn't too late for them to leave.

T.J. was at the kitchen table tinkering with his metal toy cars. She turned to him. "Guess what?"

He looked up. "What, Mum?"

"We're going to the beach tonight."

T.J.'s eyes grew big. "We are?"

She dried her hands on the tea towel. "Yes. Let's go pack."

"Yippee!"

About three hours later, their trusted guide – the GPS voice – announced their arrival in Ocean City. The last-minute weekend deal Titilope had found online was for a kid-friendly hotel right on the boardwalk.

T.J. was so wound up from the excitement that he wouldn't go to sleep. Titilope decided to take him for a walk. The night view of the boardwalk was magnificent. T.J.'s eyes grew bigger and bigger as he saw the rides, arcades, and performers along the three-mile stretch.

At the sight of the huge kites soaring in the ocean breeze, T.J. tightened his grip on her hand. "Mum, look!"

She and T.J. stood with their faces tilted upwards as people walked around them. By the time they came down from their ride on the boardwalk tram, they were both ready for bed. Titilope surprised herself by sleeping through the night.

The next morning, right after breakfast, they headed out to the beach. The night before, she'd seen magnificent views of the ocean from the tram. The clean white sand and aqua water reminded her of childhood visits to Bar Beach.

T.J. cocked his head to the side as she told him that Nigeria also had an Atlantic Ocean coastline. "Can I go see Bar Beach, too? Please."

It had been ten years since she'd visited home. She reached for T.J.'s hand. "One day, sweetie. Let's go get our beach umbrellas."

She planted their rented umbrellas and arranged their beach towels under the shade. The umbrella next to them sheltered another little boy and his mother. When their eyes met, Titilope and the woman exchanged smiles. Her little boy moved close and tossed a beach ball in T.J.'s direction.

Titilope gave T.J. a nod. He picked up the ball and threw it back. Soon, the boys chased each other all over the beach. T.J.'s carefree laughter as they played in the water brought a smile to her face.

After T.J. assured her he would stay close; she took out her mystery paperback. She got engrossed in the story until she heard T.J.'s voice. "Mum!"

She tossed the book aside and sprang up from her towel. Her heart was in her throat until her eyes found T.J. feet dug into the sand. He stood, gazing into the sky.

Titilope was relieved and annoyed at the same time. "What is it?"

"Look up, Mum. Butterflies!"

Titilope's jaw dropped at the sight of what looked like thousands of orange and black Monarch butterflies. "Where are they going?" she wondered aloud.

The woman beside her spoke up. "Mexico. It's their annual winter migration. They get to cross borders without visas or passports."

Titilope turned to face her. "Isn't it amazing how they knowwhen it's time to leave for a safer climate?"

The woman had a faraway look in her eyes. "It is. We can learn from them."

Titilope thought about her situation as she stared at the sky. She had always thought she was the kind of person who would not let anyone abuse her. She now lived in limbo in a house with few happy memories. She was neither married nor divorced. Mother of a child determined to forgive everything, co-parent with a man who seemed to have forgotten it all.

Unwilling to entertain the heavy thoughts, she abandoned her novel and joined the boys. They made themselves dizzy as they chased butterflies on the beach.

When Sunday afternoon came, neither of them wanted to go home. As they drove back to Rockville, Titilope wondered what would happen if she kept on driving. They'll probably end up in Alaska. Since she wasn't a fan of winter, not a good plan.

T.J.'s voice snapped her out of her thoughts. "Look, Mum, it's a cloud maker."

"A cloud maker?"

She turned sideways and saw smoke rising from the smokestack of a chemical plant. The big, white puff did look like a lazy cloud drifting across the sky. "It's such a beautiful cloud."

"Mum."

Titilope glanced at him through the rear-view mirror. "Yes, sweetie."

"You look beautiful when you smile. But that's only when your eyes smile too."

Thanks to expensive dental implants, she had her front teeth back. "That's a nice compliment."

"It's because you have my smile," T.J. said.

Titilope laughed. "I do have your smile."

CHAPTER TWENTY-TWO

The clothes Titilope pulled out of her closet were either dated or hung loose on her body. She glanced at her bedside clock. Tomide was coming to the house to pick up T.J. for the first of his weekend visits. She didn't want to send the wrong message by showing up at the door in her bathrobe.

She decided on a pair of dress pants and a shirt. After she had tucked in the top, she studied her face in the dresser mirror. There wasn't much she could do with her hair. Her tight curls were streaked with silver strands, and she'd left them in a short cut. She reached for her makeup bag. A layer of bronze foundation toned down the harsh look of her scars and by the time she applied lip gloss, the overall look wasn't half-bad. She and Sunbeam were headed to a volunteer fair that afternoon.

Titilope picked up her purse and headed downstairs. T.J. had just finished his breakfast when his father arrived. Tomide whistled when she opened the door. "Stunning."

Tomide was being extra. She didn't look that good. "Thanks."

"You're welcome."

After she'd given T.J. a goodbye hug, she turned to Tomide. "I'll call later to check up on him."

"No need to worry. Jordan's coming. You enjoy your weekend."

"Please call my cell phone if he needs me," she insisted.

Tomide held out a hand to his son. "Buddy, let's go."

Titilope stood by the door and watched T.J. carry on an animated conversation with his father as they walked towards his car. She knew she was doing the right thing, but it was hard to watch him go.

***

Sunbeam hung the last piece of clothing item on the rack. "Not a bad day," she said.

Titilope dusted her hands. It wasn't. They'd signed up five new volunteers at the fair and spent the past two hours sorting boxes of items donated to the Centre.

Sunbeam stretched. "My poor back. I think I'm ready for pizza now."

"Me too," Titilope said.

They took their food outside and sat on a curved stone bench near the children's playground. Titilope loved the cool, fall weather. The most beautiful thing was the colour change. One day, the leaves were green, the next, beautiful shades of orange, gold, and red.

Beside her, Sunbeam sighed with pleasure as she bit into a pizza slice. Titilope smiled. Sunbeam was a real foodie.

"There's something I need to discuss with you," she said after Sunbeam had dabbed a napkin on her lips.

"What's up?"

"I'm not sure what to do. T.J. keeps insisting that he wants his dad back at the house. He said Tomide has changed. Is it possible? My father said people don't change. That circumstances only reveal true character."

Sunbeam settled the paper plate on her lap. "My response to the question, 'Can an abusive partner change?' is yes. The answer to the question, 'Has Tomide changed enough to value you?' only he can answer."

Titilope twisted the napkin in her hand. "A part of me wants to give our marriage another chance. The other part is screaming 'run'."

"With what Tomide did to you, why would you take him back?" Sunbeam asked.

There was only one reason. "I feel as if I'm depriving T.J. of a father."

Sunbeam shook her head. "You shouldn't own that. Tomide's actions caused the separation. Your son's going to grow up. What will sustain your relationship with Tomide after he leaves home?"

She couldn't answer the question.

"You said a part of you is saying 'run'. Why?"

"If T.J. had not called for help, he would have killed me. My mother thinks the love and trust will return."

"She wants you to stay in the marriage."

"Yes. I will be the first woman in our family to leave her husband. It's just not done."

Sunbeam frowned. "Even when there's abuse?"

She nodded.

"Hmm. Have you ever heard of the pot roast story?" Sunbeam asked.

"No."

"There are different versions of it. I like this version. So, a new Jewish bride is making her first big dinner for her husband. She decides to try her hand at her mother's brisket recipe. Before she puts the meat in the oven, she cuts off the ends of the roast the way her mother always did. At dinner time, her husband tells her the brisket is delicious but adds, 'Why did you cut off the ends—those are the best part!' She answers, 'It's the way my mother always made her roast.'"

Titilope wondered how the story was going to end.

"The next week, they visit her grandmother and she prepares the famous brisket recipe, again cutting off the ends. The young bride is sure she's missing some information, so she asks her grandmother why she cuts off the ends. The grandmother says, 'It's the only way the roast would fit in my pan.'"

Sunbeam's eyes held hers. "I'm an outsider, so my words may not count. I do know just because people do things in a certain way, doesn't mean it's the best way, or it can't change."

Titilope stared at Sunbeam's wan face. There were puffy bags under her eyes. Listening to other people's pain must be draining. "You're tired," she said.

Sunbeam nodded. "I am."

"How do you keep doing this job?"

"I don't believe this path was a choice for me," Sunbeam asked. "This is the only thing that makes sense."

"I wish I felt the same way about accounting. While I like my job, I want to do something more meaningful."

Sunbeam looked thoughtfully at her. "Well, we've been thinking about offering a financial empowerment group to our clients. Too many people stay in abusive situations because of financial dependency. We need someone with your expertise to run it."

Titilope sat up. She knew how fortunate she was to have a job and a place to stay. Her sessions with Sunbeam were one of her lifelines. It was time for her to give back. "When can we start?"

CHAPTER TWENTY-THREE

Tomide scrolled through the pictures posted on Holly's Facebook page. Thanks to unsolicited updates from Jordan, her engagement to the man from Delaware was not a surprise.

It was a sign that he needed to speed things up with Titilope. Divorce papers were the last thing he wanted to receive from her.

He placed the laptop on his bed, reached for his phone and dialled her number.

"Hello?" Titilope said.

"Hi. Are you busy?"

"Yes. Do you want to speak to T.J.?"

"No. I had wanted to have a chat with you."

"Oh. Well, go ahead."

"It's not something we should talk about on the phone. I'm hoping you'll come to my place."

"We can meet at a coffeehouse," Titilope said.

"It is not the right venue for this type of conversation."

"We can use Skype," she said.

Titilope had to be curious about where he lived. "If you come over, you'll get to see where T.J. comes for his visits."

"I don't think a private meeting is a good idea."

They'd not been alone since the night of his arrest. "Titilope, I'll never hurt you again. *Please*."

"When do you want me to come?" she finally asked.

"This Friday. 7 p.m.? If that date doesn't work, we can decide on another one."

"I'll be there."

"Thank you." Tomide dropped the phone and punched the air.

***

To get rid of the cooking smells, Tomide cranked open the kitchen window. Cool air fanned his face as he sucked on a burnt finger.

He'd spent most of the day cleaning and cooking a three-course dinner. The menu was fish pepper soup, basmati rice topped with chicken gizzard stir-fry and chocolate-covered strawberries. One didn't win back a wife by treating her to a regular meal.

Over the past couple of months, he had come to accept that while his quick temper was a personality trait inherited from his father, what he did with the fiery emotion was up to him. James was right. He had to own his stupidity.

He closed the window and surveyed the candlelit room. The only thing missing was music. Tomide turned on the Bluetooth speakers. He hoped the Nigerian songs played at their wedding would remind Titilope of the two families back at home, the silent partners in their union.

The nervous feeling in Tomide's stomach grew as the minutes dragged. Heart in his mouth, he hurried towards the door when he heard a soft knock.

It was Titilope. "Sorry, I'm late," she said with a stiff smile when she walked in. "The babysitter had car issues."

He knew she'd run if he tried to give her a hug. "No, you're fine. Thanks for coming."

Titilope took off her coat. The purple and gold Ankara dress she wore looked new. A wide, gold belt emphasised her slender waist. Tomide licked his dry lips. She wouldn't have dressed up if she wasn't still interested, would she? Or perhaps she wore the outfit to show him what he was going to miss? "You look beautiful."

"Thank you."

He couldn't read her eyes. "I hope you still like eating gizzards."

"Yes." Titilope looked around the room. "This is nice."

"The owner has great taste."

Titilope's eyes settled on his face. "You said we had to talk about something important?"

"We do. But first, let's just chat and enjoy our meal."

"A meal?"

Titilope was often too tired to eat. "I'm sure you've not had your supper."

"Yes. But, I—"

"Please let me feed you," he begged.

"Tomide."

"Please."

Titilope lifted her chin. "Fine."

Relieved, he walked Titilope over to the set dining table and pulled out her chair. He poured her a glass of wine before he took his seat.

At his urging, Titilope served herself a bowl of the fish pepper soup. She gave him a surprised look after tasting it. "You made this?"

"I've become competent at many things."

Titilope took a sip from her glass of water. "I'm not sure what to say."

"Tell me what I've missed in the past six months," he said.

Titilope dropped her spoon. "Missed in my life or your son's life?"

He needed to keep her at the table until he saw the right opening. "Both. I'm sure there's a lot to tell."

She gave an exasperated sigh. "What exactly do you want from me? I didn't come here to have meaningless conversations."

"Time spent with you isn't meaningless to me."

"Since when?" Titilope asked with a raised eyebrow.

"Titilope, I'm—"

She pushed back her chair. "I need to use the bathroom."

"It's the second door on your right."

When she came back and left her food untouched, he knew he had limited time. "I've been thinking. With things going so well between us, we can start afresh."

"This is the important thing you wanted to discuss?"

"Yes. Our son is the number one priority. Why make him the product of a broken home?"

Titilope sighed. "All these years, T.J. has lived in a broken home."

He searched her face. Nothing gave him hope. "You agreed to see my counsellor."

"For our son's sake. You'll always be his father, so we need to figure out how to get along. My attendance is not about you."

He refused to concede defeat. "Would it be so bad if we got back together? Dating at our age is no walk in the park. Everyone has baggage. At least we will be familiar with ours."

Titilope looked at him as if he'd lost his mind. "You want us to get back together because it'd be difficult for you to date?"

Why couldn't he keep his foot out of his big mouth? "I now get it. I'm sorry for hurting you. For the things I did wrong and the things I didn't do right. Nothing you did or said made you deserve what I did to you."

Titilope's eyes had a faraway look as her index finger traced the raised scar by the side of her mouth. "Why did you do it?"

A sense of shame came over him. "When I did those things to you, it made me feel powerful. I also knew you wouldn't walk out of the marriage because of our background. Especially because of T.J."

Titilope gaped at him. "That's the most honest statement you've ever made to me," she said.

"Look at me. I have changed. I can still change."

She cocked her head to the side. "All those times I asked you to help out, it wasn't about who did the chores or made all the decisions. It was about you showing me some respect by listening to my needs."

"Please, give me a second chance. I know I have to work hard to regain your trust."

"We're moving," Titilope blurted out.

He gaped at her. "To where?"

"We're not leaving Rockville. We're just moving to a new place," she said.

"But…that's T.J.'s house. There's no need for you to take him elsewhere. I don't like this."

Titilope lifted her chin. "You don't have to. Our move won't impact your visits with T.J. It's my choice to make."

His desperation rose. "I still don't understand why you have to move."

"Think about it. You can stop renting and move back to your home."

Tomide shook his head. "It's not much of a home without other people in it…without you and T.J. there. Why would you want to throw away your home?"

"I'm just moving out of a brick structure," Titilope said. "You know when it stopped being my home."

He shifted in his seat. "I'm sorry."

"My mother told me a woman's accomplishments mean nothing if she couldn't keep her home. I was close to being dead and wrong."

He could feel her slipping further away from him. "Titilope, please. I love you."

She whipped her head back. "Love?"

"Yes."

His heart sank as she choked back a laugh.

"The love you offer is neither gentle nor kind." She pushed back her chair. "It's getting late."

Despite the heaviness lodged in his chest, he insisted on following her to the apartment building lobby. "Are you sure you don't want me to walk you to your car?"

Titilope shook her head. "I'll be fine."

He gave her a hopeful look. "Perhaps we can do this again soon?"

"I don't want to waste your time. Or mine. If it's something related to T.J., tell me when you pick him up, or you can call or send me an email. We don't need any more dinner dates."

"What about things related to us?"

"Tomide, there hasn't been an 'us' in years. Thanks for dinner."

Back in his apartment, Tomide dragged his feet as he went around the room. He blew out the candles one after another until the room was plunged into darkness.

CHAPTER TWENTY-FOUR

"I want to see T.J.," her mother said. "When are you bringing him to Nigeria?"

Titilope rested her head on the couch. Even though she had sole custody of T.J., she needed Tomide's permission to take their son out of the country. She was not ready for that conversation. She explained the situation to her mother.

"I'm sure Tomide will let you bring T.J. to Nigeria if you let him come back to his house. Titilope, for how much longer are you going to punish him?"

"Mummy, Tomide and I are not getting back together."

"Come again?"

"I know this is hard for you to hear, but our marriage is over."

"No! Do not tell me that nonsense."

"Would you prefer that I lie to you?"

Mummy gave a long hiss. "What is wrong with your generation of women? Must you change men like underwear? Do you think your life would have turned out well if I had left your father?"

"Daddy found himself another wife. Tomide almost killed me."

Mummy ignored her words. "If I had left you children behind your father's new wife would have used your polished skulls to drink palm wine while her children took your rightful places. I've always told you – a good mother does not run from her children's home. She stays, and she fights!"

Titilope curled her lips. "Mummy, fight for who? Fight for what? A good mother is no use to her children when she's dead."

"Stop talking about death. How many women do you know died because they stayed?"

Titilope's mind went to her childhood neighbour. "Mama Maria died," she said.

"Mama Maria fell down the stairs."

When she'd first heard the news, Titilope had pictured Daddy Maria's pot-bellied figure as he pushed his wife. "That man killed her and got away with it."

"Madam Judge and Jury, you saw the incident from your house in America?"

"He tortured her on a regular basis. It was only a matter of time."

"Titilope, these people are older than your parents. Show some respect."

"My words meant no disrespect to the dead. They only indict the living."

"I see that all the years you've spent in that place has changed you. At your age, how will you find another husband? You think someone will marry you when he discovers you sent your first husband to jail?"

"When I'm ready, I will find a man who wouldn't mind my wayward ways."

Mummy began to cry. "How will we hold our heads up?"

Even though she was an adult, Titilope knew that her mother saw the failure of her marriage to Tomide as a parenting catastrophe. "With pride. Neither of us did anything wrong."

Her mother continued to cry.

***

Titilope ran her house moving checklist through her mind as she drove to the Women's Centre for one of her private consultations. She offered them because some women were not comfortable with asking questions in a group setting.

The two-bedroom apartment she'd found was minutes away from T.J.'s day care and close to her workplace. It was the perfect fit for their life and her budget.

She'd been worried about how T.J. would handle the news. It was another change. The shiny swing sets at the apartment complex had sealed the deal. Titilope smiled to herself. The blessing of being a child.

In the back seat, T.J. hummed the Kids Club anthem to himself. He and Sunbeam became good buddies from the first day. Sunbeam had a way of making the women and children feel safe.

Titilope turned into the Centre parking lot. The relief she saw on the faces of the women after they'd sat down and discussed the financial implications of leaving abusive relationships was rewarding. The solutions they came up with were not perfect by any standard, but they were a good launch pad.

Titilope walked T.J. to the Kids Club room and handed him over to Sunbeam; she told her the woman she was scheduled to meet with had arrived. Titilope hurried off to the waiting room.

The impeccably dressed middle-aged woman with coiffed blonde hair clutched onto the handle of the gleaming Coach bag on her lap with a white-knuckled grip.

At first glance, it looked like the woman would rather be anywhere else, but there was something familiar to Titilope about the way she sat with a straight spine while her eyes darted from side to side. This woman was looking for a way out. Titilope knew how that felt.

Titilope cleared her throat. "Shirley?"

She received a tight-lipped smile. "That's me."

They exchanged handshakes. Titilope led the way to the office she used for her consultations. The women sat next to each other on a pair of overstuffed plaid chairs.

Titilope waited for Shirley to break the silence. "I don't know if you can help me," she said. "I simply don't have the means to leave."

During one of Titilope's consultations, an overwhelmed woman with spotty credit history told her that while people say leave, few are willing to take you in. Life and bills don't stop.

"I'm certainly going to try."

Shirley took a deep breath. "I never thought I would be brave enough to think of leaving my marriage."

"What helped?"

Shirley gave her a wry smile. "The AARP membership flyer I'd received in the mail."

Titilope watched as Shirley opened her purse, brought out the flyer and placed in her lap.

"As I read the congratulatory message, it struck me that fifty was around the corner. I'd been living a lie for more than half of my life. We had agreed that I wouldn't work out of the home. His wage as a commercial pilot was enough for our family of six. But, nothing was in my name. The allowance he gave me depended on his mood. I worked hard to keep him happy." Shirley sighed. "I'd stayed because of my parents, stayed for the children, stayed while he was sick, stayed because I was afraid of being alone. This week it finally occurred to me that there are worse things than being alone."

Titilope couldn't argue with that. "Before you leave we'll come up with a short-term and long-term plan. Nothing's written in stone. There are items you may be able to convert to money, jewellery, even things like reward card points; sometimes staying alive means staying creative."

She gave Shirley a safety planning pamphlet. "Please call me if you have any questions."

Shirley had tears in her eyes. "You've given me a lot to think about."

Titilope gave her an encouraging look. "Don't forget to make copies of your important financial or personal documents. And come back to see us when you're ready for the next step. Things don't have to be all figured out before you make a move."

***

"We had so much fun today," T.J. said as they headed home from the Women's Centre. "Miss Sunbeam brought us some homemade apple cider and apple cake."

"Did you say thank you?"

"Yeah." T.J. fell quiet.

Titilope slowed the car down as the traffic light changed to yellow. "What's wrong?"

"Sometimes, I feel sad for Dad. He doesn't do all the fun things we do."

Tomide was missing out on his son's life. "You can tell him all about your day during your next visit."

"I wish Dad was waiting at home. I don't want to forget," T.J. said.

"We can call him before you go to bed."

T.J. beamed. "Yes, please."

Titilope returned his smile. Today's crisis averted. She knew others would come.

CHAPTER TWENTY-FIVE

T.J.'s fifth birthday came on the eve of their big move. As usual, her mother's phone call woke Titilope up that morning. Even though they had a hard time understanding each other, Mummy always sang T.J. the birthday song in Yoruba. It was the official start to his big day.

"Thanks, grandma," T.J. said before he handed over the phone. He began jumping on her bed.

She wagged a finger at him but couldn't help but smile.

"*Ese*, Ma. We'll send your piece of cake by courier," she said to her mother.

"The cake would have grown a fungus face by the time they deliver it." There was a slight pause. "So are you still keeping this number when you move to this new place?"

"Yes, Ma. It's easier that way."

"Well, send your new address so I'll know where to find you. Unless you don't want me to have it."

Titilope had decided she'd only offer the address when her mother asked for it. "Of course I want you to have it. I'll send it in a text."

"I'll be expecting it. Titilope…"

"Ma?"

"Take care of yourself."

Titilope took a deep breath. The words painted a glimmer of what could be. "I will."

***

At T.J.'s request, Titilope called Tomide and invited him over for cake and ice cream. Earlier in the day, she and Holly took the boys out for a movie and dinner.

Titilope lit the candles on the homemade chocolate cake and brought it to the dining table.

"It's time for you to make a wish," Tomide said to their son after they sang the birthday song.

T.J.'s eyes darted between her and Tomide. "I wish that you—"

Titilope kept a smile on her face as she reached out and placed a finger across T.J.'s lips. "Sweetie, remember, if you say the wish out loud, it won't come true."

"Okay, Mum."

Her chest tightened as T.J. squeezed his eyes shut and mumbled the words under his breath.

At the end of the evening, Tomide lingered around even after she'd told him she needed get T.J. into bed.

She came back downstairs and found him in front of the boxes she'd stacked against the living room wall.

"You are moving," Tomide said as if he'd needed to hear the words aloud to believe them.

"Yes, we are."

"Titilope, please, don't leave me. I've changed. Can't you see it?"

The eyes were limited in what they could see. Titilope's mind flooded with memories as she stared at Tomide's gaunt face. In the beginning, they were T-Square. She remembered their first date, their first kiss, the day Tomide had proposed, her confident walk down the aisle on their wedding day, their joy when they brought T.J. home from the hospital. There had been many good moments, even great ones.

Although Tomide's apologies felt like salve on a wound, they were not enough to heal the emotional fractures his fists left in places deep in her body. To save her mind, she'd forgiven him. Titilope wasn't sure what kind of human being it made her, but she was unable to forget.

She walked towards the living room closet, opened it, and took out Tomide's jacket. "It's an early night for us. We have a long day tomorrow."

Tomide rubbed a hand over his head before he took his coat. She unlocked the door and held it open until he walked out and stood on the front step.

He looked hopefully at her. "Do you need me to stop by tomorrow? I can help move the heavy boxes."

She shook her head. Bunmi, Holly and Sunbeam – her tripod of helpers – were coming at different times in the day. "We're good. I'll leave the house keys inside the flower pot. Good night."

For a moment, she thought Tomide would refuse to leave. His eyes hardened, and she wondered if he would try to hurt her again. Titilope folded her arms, gripped her elbows tight and refused to give in to fear. Their eyes clashed. After a few seconds, Tomide's shoulders slumped.

"Good night." Tomide turned and walked down the porch steps.

Titilope's body shook as she locked the door. She leaned against a wall. Her calm exterior had masked a racing heart.

Titilope, he can no longer hurt you.

T.J.'s voice drifted downstairs. "Mum, are you still coming?"

Titilope looked up towards the flight of stairs. Before she came back down, she'd promised him a bedtime story. Even though T.J. no longer had nightmares, there were days when she had to stay with him until he fell asleep.

"Mum!"

Titilope headed upstairs. Never again would her child call for her in vain.

"I'm coming, sweetie. Your mum is coming."

BOOK DISCUSSION QUESTIONS

1. The central theme in Chasing Butterflies is domestic violence. Was it adequately explored?

2. What are some of the other issues explored in the book and how did they help to move the story forward?

3. Were there any notable cultural, traditions, gender, or socioeconomic factors at play in the book? If so, what? How did it affect the characters?

4. What were the dynamics of "power" between the characters? How did this impact Titilope and Tomide's marriage?

5. How did you react to Tomide's acts of contrition? Does he genuinely regret his past behaviour?

6. How does Titilope evolve throughout the book? Is there a pivotal moment which revealed her growth?

7. What did you think of the relationship between Titilope and her mother? How have the societal views on domestic violence changed across generations?

8. Do you feel Holly should have done more to help Titilope? What responsibility do we have when we find out someone is in an abusive relationship?

9. What are the signs of a healthy relationship? How are these different in an unhealthy relationship?

10.   Why is it difficult for people to leave abusive relationships?

11.   Does your community has an adequate system to protect/support victims of domestic violence and to prosecute batterers? If not, how can you help bring about a systemic change?

12.   In what ways can family and friends support those ready to leave abusive relationships?

13.   Was the book ending was appropriate? If no, how would you change it?

14.   What did you learn or take away from this book?

EXCERPT FROM DAUGHTERS WHO WALK THIS PATH

When I returned to Lagos, Kafiyah, who knew how stressed I was over the wedding, insisted that we needed a movie night. On our way to Silverbird Cinemas, she said we had to make a quick stop at her house. I had no idea that she had other plans.

"Surprise!"

Startled, I took a step back from the doorway. Kafiyah laughed as she gently pushed me into the room. Eniayo and a beaming Ekanem were among the small group of women. Balloons with wedding bells and streamers were everywhere. Eniayo handed me a sash with "Mrs. Nwosu" printed on it to wear over my clothes. Kafiyah had organized a surprise wedding shower.

Ekanem and I flew into each other's arms. I had not seen her since her wedding. She was glowing.

"Ekanem, you came!"

"Bride-to-be!" Ekanem said. "You know I would not miss this for the world."

Later Kafiyah teased, "Okay now. Morayo, let us see what Ekanem bought you." When I unwrapped Ekanem's present, I recognized the gift box. It was from one of the exclusive lingerie stores on Victoria Island.

Ekanem smiled at me. "Morayo, do you remember that conversation we had about getting ammunition for our marriage arsenals? I bought you some essentials. I know Kachi has been waiting." My neck grew warm when everybody started laughing.

Lifting the tissue, I saw a matching pink silk and lace bra and panties. The women all ooh'd and aah'd as they passed the lingerie around.

"That, my friends, is known in select married circles as the grenade," Ekanem said. "Small but mighty, guaranteed to produce an instant reaction."

"Eky Baby!" Kafiyah said with a laugh.

"Trust me, Kaffy; I am a true Efik woman. My mother shared the notes she took down inside the fattening room."

"Morayo, please bring out the next item for viewing," Ekanem said. It was a red silk chiffon teddy with shiny gold silk threads.

"Aha!" Ekanem exclaimed. "The Tear Gas. Grown men have been known to weep at the sight of this little mama."

Eniayo's face was now almost as red as the teddy. "Ekanem," I laughed, "I beg you, please don't kill my sister."

"Eniayo, close your eyes," Kafiyah commanded. Eniayo covered her eyes with her fingers, but I saw her smiling anyway. After all, her Tunde was patiently waiting for her to finish school, and someday she would be unwrapping such gifts too.

I pulled out the last item from the box. It was a backless lilac nightgown with a plunging neckline and a matching robe. Ekanem bowed her head. "Last but definitely not the least. Behold, the Rocket Launcher M4 Special Edition. The ticket to that guaranteed honey pot in the moon."

"Honestly, Ekanem, you missed your calling," Titi from head office said. "You should be on stage doing stand-up comedy."

"Or selling lingerie to premium ladies of the night along Allen Avenue!" Kafiyah said.

Ekanem narrowed her eyes at Kafiyah. "Kaffy, I guess you will be public relations officer for the lingerie business?" Ekanem laughed when Kafiyah visibly shuddered. "My sisters, it is good to know I have some options if this banking career becomes too much for me to handle. Very soon, I won't find more family members with money to deposit at our bank!"

The rest of the evening passed quickly as we ate, laughed, played some games, and danced.

On our way out of the house, we went to greet Kafiyah's aunty, Hajia. "Hajia, thank you for your hospitality."

Hajia wove her dainty fingers in the air. "It is nothing, my dear. I am happy you enjoyed your evening."

As we walked out of the room, Hajia called my name. "Morayo."

I turned. "Yes, Hajia."

"I would recommend that you start with the Tear Gas," she said with a shy smile.

Ekanem's hearty laughter echoed throughout the house.

ACKNOWLEDGEMENTS

First thanks to my Lord Jesus Christ for the gifts of life and inspiration. Each story I write takes me on a heart journey. I remain grateful for His grace and faithfulness.

To Oladele and our children, Oluwafikunmi, Ifeoluwakishi and Oluwademilade, thanks for the love, joy, and stability you bring to my life.

Sincere thanks to my family and friends, near and far, who support my dreams through prayers and encouragement. I appreciate every one of you.

Thanks to my village – Oyindamola Orekoya, Unoma Nwankwor, Adenike Campbell-Fatoki, Chika Unigwe, Melanie Freeman, Karen Rodgers, Debrah Pallister, Rashidat Fawehinmi-Raji and Victor Ehikhamenor for the invaluable critique and support.

Dear reader, it's an honour to share my stories with you. Thank you.

ABOUT THE AUTHOR

Yejide Kilanko was born in Ibadan, Nigeria. She is a writer of poetry, fiction and a therapist in children's mental health. Her debut novel, *Daughters Who Walk This Path*, was first published by Penguin Canada in April 2012. Kilanko lives with her family in Ontario, Canada. Please visit www.yejidekilanko.com

Printed in Great Britain
by Amazon